"Ava, when the shooting starts, I need you to dive down."

"Okay. But what about you?"

"I'll be fine."

Oliver kept zigzagging, but the car stayed with them, the driver not moving a muscle but keeping the car close.

"We're going to keep moving and hope they'll either back off...or play chicken with us."

But the vehicle advanced and tapped the back bumper.

"Now they're getting serious," Oliver said.

* * *

With over seventy books published and millions in print, **Lenora Worth** writes award-winning romance and romantic suspense. Three of her books finaled in the ACFW Carol Awards, and her Love Inspired Suspense novel *Body of Evidence* became a *New York Times* bestseller. Her novella in *Mistletoe Kisses* made her a *USA TODAY* bestselling author. Lenora goes on adventures with her retired husband, Don, and enjoys reading, baking and shopping...especially shoe shopping.

Books by Lenora Worth

Love Inspired Suspense

Military K-9 Unit

Rescue Operation

Classified K-9 Unit

Tracker
Classified K-9 Unit Christmas
"A Killer Christmas"

Rookie K-9 Unit

Truth and Consequences
Rookie K-9 Unit Christmas
"Holiday High Alert"

Capitol K-9 Unit

Proof of Innocence
Capitol K-9 Unit Christmas
"Guarding Abigail"

Visit the Author Profile page at Harlequin.com for more titles.

RESCUE OPERATION

LENORA WORTH

HARLEQUIN® LOVE INSPIRED® SUSPENSE

Special thanks and acknowledgment are given to Lenora Worth for her contribution to the Military K-9 Unit miniseries.

Recycling programs for this product may not exist in your area.

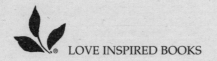

® LOVE INSPIRED BOOKS

ISBN-13: 978-1-335-49052-0

Rescue Operation

Copyright © 2018 by Harlequin Books S.A.

www.Harlequin.com

Printed in U.S.A.

When the host goeth forth against thine enemies,
then keep thee from every wicked thing.
—Deuteronomy 23:9

To the men and women of the US military.
We respect and love all of you, and we will be forever
grateful for your dedication and sacrifice. And especially
to Wilberto Garcia, my air force son-in-law. Stay safe!

ONE

Ignoring the tilt and rumble of the HH-60G Pave Hawk helicopter about to hoist her down below and the dark thunderstorm approaching from the west, Senior Airman Ava Esposito adjusted the sturdy harness sleeves around the black nylon sling holding the sixty-five-pound yellow Lab that was about to rappel with her. Roscoe's trusting eyes followed her while he hovered close to her chest, always eager to work.

"That's right. It's showtime. We've got to find that little boy."

Roscoe wouldn't understand, but they were armed and ready for anything or anyone they might confront in the dense woods that belonged to Canyon Air Force Base in the Hill Country of Texas. This reserve, mostly used for training, covered hundreds of acres and could hide a person for weeks if not months. Right now, she had to find a lost little boy and watch her back for a serial killer who'd escaped from prison in the spring and was reported to be back in these woods. Boyd Sullivan, known as the Red Rose Killer because he always left one red rose to warn his victims and one after he'd killed them, was a dangerous, deranged man. He'd killed five people over two years ago in his hometown of Dill, Texas. He'd been put in prison for those killings, but he'd escaped and made his way to Canyon Air Force Base to kill again. Two of those he'd murdered had been friends and coworkers of Ava's. But he hadn't left it at that. He'd also let out two hundred or so dogs from the Military Working Dog K-9 kennels located on the base. Let them out to run wild. Some that had suffered PTSD were still roaming around these woods. Now seven-year-old Turner Johnson, the son of Colonel Gregory and Mrs. Marilyn Johnson, had gone missing from his backyard this morning. The boy was up against wild animals, dogs with PTSD and a se-rial killer who wouldn't think twice about nabbing the kid for leverage.

Her focus humming on high alert, Ava checked her weapons and equipment one more time. Then she patted the alert K-9 on his furry head. "Ready?"

Roscoe woofed his reply.

Nodding, she scooted to the open side of the chopper and let her booted feet dangle out, Roscoe's warm breath hitting the inch or so of skin she had showing outside of her heavy camo uniform, protective combat vest, knap-sack and M16 rifle.

Above her, a crew member adjusted the carabiner hold-ing the pulleys that would hoist both Ava and Roscoe so they could rappel down, each with their own pulley to hold them securely together.

Halfway down, she listened to the chopper's crew re-porting back and forth while she hovered and checked below. Nothing but heavy woods, scattered rocks and hills, and a hint of clay here and there. But somewhere out there was a lost, scared little seven-year-old boy.

"Hold on, Roscoe."

Something whizzed past her like a gnat. But even with

the chopper's bellowing roar all around her, she heard the ding of metal hitting metal.

And then she saw it. The ricochet of a bullet hitting the fuselage. Someone was shooting at them.

The chopper banked left, causing Ava to shift on the rope. Above her, the gunner motioned for her to come back up.

Then she heard the pilot. "We need to abort."

"Negative," she said through the mic attached to her helmet. "I'm going in."

With that, she steadied herself and, along with Roscoe, hurried the few yards to the ground, relieved to see that team member Chad Watson came down seconds after her. Ava dropped, unhooked the harnesses and turned on a low crouch, ready to return fire.

"Chad, take Custer to the south and wait," she said, referring to Chad's K-9 partner. "Start your search there."

"We have a situation here, ma'am," he reported back.

"*I* have a situation, and I can handle it," she replied. "And Buster will cover me, right, Buster?"

"Affirmative, ma'am. I'm about twenty yards behind you."

Buster Elliott, all two hundred and fifty pounds of him, was with Security Forces. He'd been assigned to watch her six while she searched for the boy. Good thing, too.

More shots hit all around her, and Buster returned fire while the chopper hovered.

"Don't engage," she warned the gunner and Buster through the mic. "The boy could be down here."

Heavy footsteps stomped through the woods, echoing toward her. Ava belly-crawled to an outcropping of shrubs and rocks, Roscoe doing the same behind her.

Then she lifted up to a crouch.

Letting out a gasp, Ava stared at the man standing a few feet away with what looked like an M4 aimed at her.

The Red Rose Killer.

He hadn't wasted any time in confronting her. Now her only concern was for the boy. Did this monster already have Turner?

"I'm not here to hurt you," Boyd Sullivan said, anger and annoyance singing through each word, his blue eyes cold and icy. Backing away, he held his rifle trained on her, but his gaze darted back and forth. "Tell your man to back off."

Ava lifted her fist to tell Buster to hold fire. Then she held her rifle trained on the tall blond man wearing an old beret. "What do you want?"

Roscoe hadn't moved from his alert, but the big dog's low growl indicated he was very aware of this intruder. Buster should still be nearby, too. Ava knew he'd have her back and even as big as he was, he'd use stealth while he kept his rifle trained on Boyd Sullivan. He'd also fire if he had to.

"Pretend you never saw me," Sullivan said. "That's all I need right now."

Ava didn't dare let the killer know she recognized him or ask if he'd seen the boy, in case he wasn't aware. And she didn't get a chance to react any further.

Bullets pierced the air again in a rapid explosion. Ava hit the ground and ordered Roscoe to do the same. Buster returned fire and took off through the woods, all the while communicating with the hovering chopper above.

And then it was over. The woods went silent. Ava lifted her head and tugged at her rifle. Still lying low, she adjusted her aim. But Boyd Sullivan, the man known as the Red Rose Killer, had disappeared back into the woods.

The shooter had covered his escape.

* * *

"You saw the Red Rose Killer?"

Rain flowed like a dam had opened all around FBI Special Agent Oliver Davison. Tired and in need of about two days of uninterrupted sleep, Oliver stared at the tougher-than-nails woman who'd called him to these woods to report what she'd just been through. Tall, red-headed, brown-eyed and clearly in no mood to bicker with him, Senior Airman Ava Esposito appeared to have things under control.

A Security Forces Military Working Dog handler who was used to rappelling out of choppers alongside her K-9 partner and working with Search-and-Rescue to find injured or compromised troops the world over, she didn't seem the least bit fazed by the gully washer trying to knock them to their knees. Or the fact that she'd come face-to-face with a notorious killer.

Come face-to-face and lived, at that. Which was why Oliver had a hard time believing her.

The Red Rose Killer didn't mess around. Boyd Sullivan hadn't made it through basic training and never had a relationship last longer than a few months. The man had gone off the deep end in a way that had become very personal to Oliver. Sullivan had killed five people in Dill, Texas, where he'd grown up, including Madison Ackler, who had been Oliver's fiancée at the time of her death. His fiancée…but she'd also been involved with Boyd Sullivan when she'd died.

Oliver had been in on the hunt and the arrest for those killings two years ago and he'd been relieved when Sullivan was sent to prison. But the Red Rose Killer had escaped in April and apparently made it to the base and allegedly killed his Basic Training commander, Chief Master Sergeant Clint Lockwood, two overnight-shift

K-9 trainers and a commissary cook, whose ID he had used to get him on and off the base. He'd also let most of the K-9s go in an attempt to distract the entire Security Forces unit. They'd been searching for him for months.

"I can't believe this," he said, voicing his doubts. Oliver still remembered what the Red Rose Killer was capable of.

Ava nodded, her camouflage uniform weighed down with a backpack, weapons and equipment. All wet now. "Believe it, Special Agent. I'm still in shock myself." Shaking water off her helmet, she added, "We'd expected this but I didn't think he'd show up the minute my boots hit the ground."

"Where?" Oliver asked, ready to get down to business. He had to admit, she looked a little shook-up but she was holding things together. Meanwhile, he had to tell himself to stay calm.

Pointing to a thicket behind him, she said, "Right over there."

Lightning flashed like a spotlight, followed by a rolling thunder that stomped through the trees and shook the woods.

Figured everything would start happening during one of the worst storms of late summer.

After four years of living and working in the San Antonio FBI Bureau, Oliver still hated these Texas downpours and the humidity that always surrounded them. At times like this, he missed the New York town where he'd grown up.

Pushing away memories, Oliver focused on Ava Esposito, questions rolling through his mind.

Leaning in so he could make himself heard over the thunder and lightning putting on a show over the forest reserve behind the base, he stared at the stubborn woman standing beside him.

"So, Senior Airman Esposito, you're sure the person you saw was Boyd Sullivan—the Red Rose Killer?"

"Yes," she said on an impatient note, brown eyes making him think of how much he wanted a cup of coffee right now. "First, we were shot at when we rappelled out of the chopper. And now this."

"Who is *we*?"

"Myself, K-9 handler Chad Watson and Security Forces officer Buster Elliott. The crew wanted us to abort, but we were halfway down, so we dropped and spread out. The shots continued while the chopper circled. But our gunner couldn't fire, because of the concerns for the boy."

Turner Johnson, the seven-year-old who'd gone missing while playing in his backyard this morning. The boy's high-ranking parents were beside themselves because the whole area had been warned about an escaped convict possibly being in the vicinity. Just one more wrinkle that concerned Oliver more than a little bit. The killer had reportedly left the base a few days ago but they'd had signs over the last couple days that he might be back in the area. Now they had proof. But they also had to search for a rambunctious kid known for sneaking into the woods behind his house.

"And what happened next?"

"We hit the dirt, returned a round of fire and the shooting stopped long enough for me to come upon Sullivan. He told me to hold off my man, so he must have seen Buster and Chad rappelling down behind me and he must have known that Chad went in the other direction. Then the shooting started up again, and he got away. I called you immediately and then we went about our business. Buster searched for Sullivan but to no avail, and Chad went off on another search grid. Roscoe alerted in this spot a few minutes later."

"You were right to call me."

"Yes, but now I'm regretting that decision. We've got a whole team on the alert and you're wasting time *not* believing me."

"I'm trying to get a handle on this. Go on."

Taking a breath, she squared her shoulders. "Roscoe started digging and I tried to follow his lead until you got here. But I can assure you the man I saw was Sullivan. I certainly know his face and I know what he's capable of doing."

Oliver saw a slight tremble forming on her lips. Delayed reaction. He had to keep her talking, however. "What happened between you two? Did you try to detain him?"

Ava gave him a look that asked, *So this is how you're gonna play this?*

"Sullivan held an M4 on me. He was wearing a tight uniform that obviously didn't belong to him and a black tam. He looked me in the eye and said, 'I'm not here to hurt you.'"

Motioning behind them, she said, "He also told me to pretend I'd never seen him and ordered me to call off my guard. I didn't get to question him since more gunfire erupted and Sullivan used the distraction to get away."

"Just like that?"

"Yes, just like that," she said, grinding out each word. "Last time we saw him, he was headed west."

Oliver felt a headache coming on. His black water-resistant FBI jacket sparkled with fat raindrops. "But he told you he wasn't shooting at *you*? And he just walked away?"

"He told me he wasn't going to hurt me," she said

again, her porcelain skin damp and dewy. "What part of *I stood face-to-face with the Red Rose Killer* don't you understand?"

"I don't understand any of this," Oliver replied, matching her inch for inch since she was almost as tall as him, his eyes holding hers in a stubborn standoff that not even a torrential rain could stop. "The man killed five people in his hometown and he's gone on a killing spree on this base throughout the summer. Not to mention he has a whole target list that he *wants* to kill. And we have reason to believe he also killed Airman Drew Golosky a few days ago in order to get his uniform and ID for base access. But he tells you he's not going to hurt you?"

"Yes, Special Agent Davison," Ava Esposito said again, aggravation deeply embedded in her words. "But someone did shoot at me and then Boyd Sullivan headed into the woods. I think that shooter, along with my K-9 partner and Buster watching my back, saved me."

Stomping water off her boots, she added, "The shooter must have been covering Sullivan. If that's the case, then he has some help. Which we've suspected all along. So let me get back to my work, and you go find the Red Rose Killer and whoever else is out there."

He wanted to find Boyd Sullivan, all right. Especially since he had a personal beef with the man. Most of the investigative team knew Oliver's history with Boyd Sullivan, even if they didn't bring it up. Oliver was the only one who knew the whole truth about Madison's past, and that she'd been briefly involved with Sullivan in high school and again a few years ago when she'd been dating Oliver. Her murder was still too personal for Oliver to talk about, and he couldn't risk being pulled off the case because of his personal interest. His SAC had approved his coming here, with the stipulation that he didn't have a personal vendetta. But how could he not?

Needing the whole picture, he asked, "Did you send your K-9 partner after him?"

"Roscoe alerted on this cave," she replied, pointing to the jagged four-foot-high rock face covered in bushes. "I kept him here because I was concerned about getting shot before I could locate the missing boy who might be inside."

A little boy missing in six hundred acres of dense thicket overgrown with clusters of trees and heavy brush. A place where dark caves and craggy hills and rocky bluffs made searching that much harder. A place where all types of predators, from poisonous snakes to wild animals of all shapes and sizes, lurked about.

Oliver worried about the worst kind of predator. The Red Rose Killer. He'd have no qualms about killing a child.

"But you haven't found the boy?"

Rain rolled off her helmet while disappointment and annoyance singed hot through her pretty eyes. "No, Turner Johnson was not inside the cave, so obviously I haven't found the boy. But I will. Roscoe is never wrong."

Oliver squinted into the wet, chilly woods. All around them, Security Forces, the Office of Special Investigations and the Military Working Dog handlers moved like hulking shadows while choppers whirled overhead. Crime-scene techs searched for evidence and bullet fragments or shell casings. Boyd Sullivan was out there somewhere. Probably long gone by now, however, since the woods had become overrun with air force personnel.

Oliver looked toward the heavens. "A missing seven-year-old and a serial killer on the loose. In the same woods. This is not good. So not good."

Her hostile gaze affirmed that summary. "No, and I really need to get back to Roscoe and his find."

Touching her arm, he glanced at the patient golden-coated Labrador retriever and said, "I understand you want to explore Roscoe's discovery. I'm anxious to catch up with the team searching for Boyd Sullivan. But I need to ask you a few more questions."

She glared at him for a moment and then checked on the K-9 eager to dig in the mud. "I've told you what happened and now I'm going to do what I came here to do. Because whatever's buried here might give us a clue to find the boy."

Special Agent Oliver Davison stared at Ava, skepticism heavy in his green eyes. The man obviously didn't believe a word of what she'd just told him. And he was seriously beginning to get on her already singed nerves.

But he did have a point. Why had Sullivan allowed her to live when he'd killed so many people already?

He'd been sent to prison for those killings a few years ago. He wanted revenge, and he was willing to kill anyone who stood in his way. He was armed and dangerous, and yes, she'd let him get away. That didn't sit well with Ava, but she had to focus on the mission at hand.

Even while the creepiness factor made her want to take off and track the killer.

Sullivan earned his name because he always left a red rose and a note stating "I'm coming for you" to warn his victims, and another note stating "Got you" after he'd killed them. Four other base personnel were targeted, so the base had been on high alert all summer. Boyd had a way on and off the base and Ava believed, along with her team members, that he was hiding out in these woods and using uniforms and IDs from some of the other airmen he'd killed to keep up the charade.

Now she'd seen the killer with her own eyes and this agent doubted her and wanted to waste her time while a child could get caught in the cross fire. Glaring up at him, Ava saw something besides a steely determination in the special agent's green eyes.

Sadness. Then it hit her. He'd been involved with one of the victims from Dill. She didn't know the whole story, but rumors had circulated. Now was not the time to go into that, however.

"I need to get back to work," she said on a calm note, hoping to cut him some slack. "Roscoe's waiting to do his job."

"Just a few more details," he insisted, a stubborn glint in his eyes.

Remembering how her heart had gone haywire earlier, Ava thought about Boyd Sullivan's weird reaction to finding her there. Dressed in dirty, ill-fitting camouflage, he'd looked wild and disoriented, but he'd been carrying an arsenal of weapons.

Thinking about it now, she held herself rigid so she wouldn't get the shakes.

To stay focused, she stared at Oliver Davison, taking in how his green eyes matched the lush foliage all around them. "Buster went after Sullivan and tracked him, but lost him. Chad and Custer had an alert in another area due east. They couldn't make it back in time."

"Why didn't you send Roscoe after Sullivan?"

"And risk losing my partner *and* the boy's location? I sent Buster after Sullivan because I was afraid the boy might still be in the area. Turner Johnson is my first obligation."

Oliver pushed water off his thick dark hair. "So you let Boyd Sullivan slip through your fingers?"

"I don't like your tone, Special Agent."

"Well, I don't like losing a wanted serial killer, Airman Esposito."

"I'm here to find the boy. It's your job to track Boyd Sullivan, and apparently you haven't been very successful so far."

"Ouch, that hurt."

She almost laughed, but this was not funny. She understood how he wanted to get his man, but he was stepping on her toes right now. "I'm going to see what Roscoe has found, if you don't mind. You have a whole team here to search for Sullivan."

"I guess I'm dismissed."

She turned in time to see the flare of both anger and admiration in his interesting eyes. "You could say that, yes."

But he called out to her. "Hey, if Boyd Sullivan wasn't shooting at you, then who was, and why?"

TWO

Ava wanted to find the answer to Oliver Davison's questions, too, but right now she had to get back to *her* search. Not only was she concerned for the boy's safety, but Turner's parents wielded a lot of clout. The whole base was on high alert over this. The negative press wouldn't be good either.

After Mr. FBI left, Chad Watson came bounding up, his blond hair glistening wet, K-9 Custer sloshing through the mud ahead of him. Chad had transferred from Security Forces to the Military Working Dog program and now excelled at his job.

"Nothing on the alert we had. Custer did a thorough grid but didn't find anything regarding the boy." Then he showed her a paper evidence bag inside his uniform pocket. "But we did find this."

Ava stared down into the open pocket, her hand shielding the bag from the rain. A Buff. A navy floral headband which could have gotten lost by anyone hiking through these woods, but it did look feminine. "Keep it bagged so we can give it to Forensics," she said, deciding anything could be evidence.

Chad nodded. "I'll take Custer and do a grid to the north."

"Good idea. While you do that, we'll dig here," she

said. Then she radioed Buster. "Need you back at the search site."

Ava gave Roscoe the order and they both worked beside him, using their gloved hands to sift through the mud and dirt surrounding the cave, but to no avail. Yet Roscoe didn't let it go. He pawed and whined and stared at her for his next command.

"Nothing," she said. After radioing in her request and cordoning off the area where they'd already dug, they kept searching and calling out for Turner Johnson, going back over the area in every direction. But the boy didn't respond and Roscoe didn't alert anywhere else. Her partner returned to stand firm in front of the cave, so she checked inside again but didn't find anything.

"Roscoe, boy, I know you are smart and there is something here, but it's getting dark and we're gonna have to let the next shift take over."

Roscoe gave her a solemn stare and then looked toward the cave again. But he was so well trained, he didn't make a move.

Thirty minutes later, the storm raged on, thunder and lightning indicating it had stalled over these woods, lessening visibility to a minimum.

Ava got a message to return to the base with Security Forces. It was too risky to bring in the chopper but the night shift would hike in from the trail and take over.

"I don't want to leave," she said, rain slashing at her with a needle-sharp consistency. "It's getting dark. I'm so worried about that little boy."

Buster stood like a dark statue, his deep brown eyes on her. "I can stay and help the relief team, ma'am."

"It's okay, Buster. We've got a fresh second shift arriving. They'll set up camp and keep searching as long as they can. We all know the first forty-eight hours are crucial in finding a missing child."

"And it's only been a few hours," Buster replied. "With this storm, things go up a notch."

So much could happen. The boy could slip and fall into rushing water from the nearby rivers and creeks. Flash floods were common in this area during storms. She prayed he'd found a safe place to shelter. Prayed he was still alive. At least the kid was a Cub Scout. Maybe his training would kick in. The temperature would be warm, but with this rain everything took on a chill.

"We have to rest and regroup tomorrow. The Amber Alert is out on the whole base and the surrounding area. The second shift is already arriving, and Chad is briefing them."

"What if—"

"I know what you're thinking," she said to the gentle giant. "What if Boyd Sullivan has the boy and that's why he didn't shoot us? What if he had to get back to the kid?"

"Yes," Buster said. "Exactly. He sure did run fast when those other bullets started flying."

"Yes, he did, didn't he?" Ava wasn't sure if the bullets had been for Boyd or her, or both. But her gut told her the shooter was covering Sullivan. Maybe he didn't kill Ava because he'd seen the heavy activity in the woods and it was too messy and risky.

Whatever his reasons, she thanked God she was still alive.

When the second shift had arrived and she'd updated the head of Security Forces, Captain Justin Blackwood, Ava trudged to the trail and got in an SF SUV with Roscoe safe in a kennel and returned to the base, exhausted and disappointed.

"I'm going back out first thing in the morning," she told lead handler Master Sergeant Westley James after she'd updated several team members in the MWD training center conference room. "I promised Mrs. Johnson I wouldn't give up on finding her son."

"I agree," her boss said, his blue eyes giving away nothing as the others filed out. "We're running out of time on the boy and we now know Boyd Sullivan could be living in those woods. Which means our earlier reports on his whereabouts were wrong. He's back in the area."

"Yes, we are running out of time," a deep voice said from the doorway of the conference room. "And now you're in danger, too, Senior Airman Esposito."

Ava whirled to find a very wet, haggard-looking FBI agent staring over at them. "Special Agent Davison, I take it you didn't find Boyd Sullivan after all?"

Oliver looked as defeated as she felt. "Nope, and that storm and a pitch-dark sky brought everything to a grinding halt. But we found signs of what looked like camping areas in two different locations, so we bagged what could be evidence. I'm going to grab a shower in the locker room and then, Airman Esposito, I'd like a word with you on how we can coordinate our searches tomorrow."

"I'm off to get a shower, too," she said, thinking she'd head in the opposite direction of him. "Meet me back here at 19:00?"

He glanced at his fancy watch. "Sounds good."

Westley James cut his gaze from Ava to the FBI agent but didn't say a word. Then he grabbed his beret. "I'm going home now to be with Felicity."

Staff Sergeant Felicity Monroe, a former K-9 handler and now the base photographer and Westley's wife, was still considered a target of the Red Rose Killer. He'd want to make sure she was safe, of course.

"Give her my best, sir."

"Will do. And, Ava, Agent Davison is right. You're in

danger now, too. Sullivan might have let you go today, but you're on his radar now. He can't leave any loose threads."

Ava nodded and turned to go, conscious of Oliver Davison's green-eyed gaze following her every step.

"How 'bout we get out of here and go to the Winged Java?" she said once she was clean and dry, her damp hair curled up under her navy beret, her blue T-shirt clean and fresh against her ABUs.

"Ah, the notorious coffee shop where flyboys and air force cadets hang out and brag about their daring deeds?" he asked, his dark hair shimmering and glossy from his shower, the scent of soap all around him. "I imagine you have a lot to brag about."

Actually, she just wanted to get away from prying eyes and go over the details of the Boyd Sullivan case and how it would interfere with finding Turner Johnson.

"I don't like braggadocios."

"Did you really just say *braggadocios*?"

She laughed. "I can teach you a lot of new words."

"I suppose you can. Let's go."

She started toward the door, her keys in her hand, and tried really hard to forget that he was good-looking and overconfident. He'd changed to a white button-down shirt and dark slacks, which made him stand out like a stranger in a spaghetti Western.

He beat her to the door and opened it. "I'll drive."

Ava scooted around him and out the door. "I'll meet you there."

"Afraid to ride with me, Esposito?"

"No, Special Agent. I can go home straight from there. Since we have special permission to take our K-9 partners home until the Red Rose Killer is caught, I have Roscoe to consider."

"Of course." He nodded and jingled his key fob. "I'll see you in a few."

The Winged Java was a legendary coffee shop, just as Oliver Davison had mentioned, but it was also a great place to relax and grab a burger or the best pizza in Texas, according to Ava's way of thinking. And because she was hungry and needed coffee and maybe a slice of pie, she grinned when she pulled up in the parking lot.

"Roscoe, guess where we are?"

Roscoe loved the Winged Java, too, since K-9s were as welcome here as humans. Maybe even more so. The manager always gave her treats to give to Roscoe at her discretion. Ava could leave him in the temperature-controlled kennel in her SUV, but she preferred having him with her whenever she could.

Normally Military Working Dogs didn't go home with their handlers, but base commander Lieutenant General Nathan Hall had given them special permission to keep the seasoned K-9s with them because of the brutal murders on base. Over the last few months, she'd gotten used to having Roscoe around. And so had several of the base restaurants. Because he was trained in search and rescue, Roscoe was more acclimated socially than the German shepherds and Belgian Malinois that did heavy battle duty, but he still had to be handled carefully in social situations.

Checking Roscoe's uniform, a vest that identified him as a Military Working Dog so people would use caution when approaching him, Ava knew Roscoe would be on his best behavior.

But she wasn't so sure about the intense man waiting for her in a corner booth. Taking a breath after spotting Oliver Davison through the window, she stared at the giant white coffee mug mural on the front of the building in an effort to stall this meeting.

Flanked by two wings that were lit up with red, white and blue lights, the cup showcased a chevron emblem. Above the cup, the café's name was done in black. The Winged Java. Inside, the walls were covered with photos and posters lauding the pride this area held for the base and the air force, some of those photos capturing shots of the Military Working Dog handlers and their dogs in training and on the job.

After sitting there for five minutes, dread weighing her down because she didn't want this man interfering in her job or her life, Ava went in and faced Oliver Davison.

"I ordered two coffees," he said, the scent of something clean and tropical hitting the air as she settled into the booth across from him. "I've seen you inhaling it in the break room."

That comment garnered him a concentrated stare. "Spying on me?"

"No, just part of the job to stay on the alert and observe people. I mean, we've never been officially introduced but you are always around."

She'd whizz through the break room with a dare to anybody who messed with her, but she'd stop on a dime to pet a dog or talk to a fellow handler. And when she smiled…

She was not smiling now, he noticed. "Does that bother you? Me always being around, that is?"

"Should it?"

She didn't look at the menu when the waitress showed up with their coffee and asked for their orders. "Cheeseburger, medium rare, with fries on the side. No mayo but loaded down."

"A woman who knows her own mind," the waitress said through a chuckle. "And for you, sir?"

Oliver glanced at the menu and looked up at Ava. "I'll have what she's having and hope I can eat the whole thing."

"Try to keep up," the freckled older woman said. Then she greeted Roscoe where he lay beside the booth with a "Hey, boy," before she walked away with a smile.

"They seem to know you here," Oliver said.

Ava's brown eyes turned a warm honey pecan. "I come here a lot."

"I've been in a few times," he offered. "But I just get a lot of stares."

"I wonder why that is," she quipped, obviously enjoying making him squirm a bit.

"Maybe they know I'm an outsider, or, worse, a dreaded Yankee from New York. Took the San Antonio Bureau a while to adjust to my accent and my bluntness."

"*We* don't judge that way," she said through a wry grin. "But they might wonder about the suit thing in the heat of summer. Here we go with jeans, T-shirts and boots when we have downtime."

"Hey, I left my coat and tie in the car, and I have a pair of boots."

"I'm guessing you've never taken 'em out of the box."

Feeling sheepish, he lowered his head. "Once… maybe."

After their food came, he leaned back and stared at the table. "What a day. Sorry you didn't find the boy."

Ava stared down at the table and then checked the parking lot. Like him, she probably never let her guard down. "I talked to Marilyn Johnson when we got back to base. The poor woman is distraught. Their only child. She's afraid Turner could have been taken but he has gone into the woods beyond their yard without permission before."

"We couldn't be sure he was still around," Oliver reminded her. "And now the killer has gone to ground. If he has the kid, this goes from bad to worse."

"We have people still looking but, like you, they had to slow things until this storm passes." Staring out into the light drizzle, she added, "I don't want to think about that little boy out in the woods in the rain and dark."

"Same with the Red Rose Killer," Oliver replied. "I sure don't want to think about him out there with the boy. He could use the boy for leverage or as a way out of here. I'm going back out first thing tomorrow."

"Me, too."

"He's left way too many threatening notes and now he's back to make good on them," Oliver said. "He's getting onto the base with other people's IDs and, just as we've suspected, he obviously has an accomplice, based on what happened today. He has to have found a way from the reserve to the base, which is probably how he got away again this time. I'm praying the boy isn't with him."

"I'm hoping the boy had the good sense to hide," Ava replied, her tone full of worry. "We couldn't get a bead on Sullivan. The chopper couldn't land in that dense area, but they did a good job of dropping us," she said. "I hope the night crew can make some headway since I didn't get anywhere."

"You're good at your job," Oliver said. "That's obvious." Then he made a snap decision. "Save the air force some money and let me give you a ride tomorrow. Unless, of course, you really do want to rappel down a rope dangling from a hovering forty-million-dollar chopper again."

"Hmm." Surprise on her pretty face, she held her

hands up in the air and moved them up and down as if weighing something. "Those are my only choices?"

He laughed at that. She had a quick wit and a no-nonsense attitude that was refreshing. "You don't give an inch, do you?"

"Should I?"

"I'm trying to figure that out," he said, his eyes holding hers again. "And…while we're at it, tell me why you wanted to have this conversation away from the office, and maybe tell me a little bit about you, too."

She matched his gaze and shook her head. "I'm not sure myself why I decided to hold this meeting here, but you know how things go. Prying eyes and listening ears. I'm working to move up a rank. Right now, it's hard to trust anyone. My team is solid but we've had some major leaks with the so-called Anonymous Blogger. But one thing I can tell you—I'm here to discuss the investigation, not share the intimate details of my life. Especially with a man who seems to read people with an ease that leaves them floundering."

"Me?" Impressed that *she* could read him so well, he shrugged. "Again, part of the job. I'm curious about what makes people tick." Then to gain her trust, he leaned in. "In your case, I'd really like to get to know you. Your team is so tight, it's been hard for me to break through."

"And you think I'll be the one to crack?"

"No, I think you're the toughest one of all. But I'd appreciate knowing more about you."

Looking skeptical, she shrugged right back at him. "Not much to tell. I decided in high school to join the air force. I took a helicopter ride once out on Galveston beach when I was a preteen and fell in love. That, coupled with not knowing what to do with my life, made me want to travel and find adventure. Didn't take much from there to want to be a chopper pilot."

"Can you fly one?"

"I was headed that way but my plans changed. I love what I do now and if I work hard I just might make it to staff sergeant."

"I'd like to hear more of that story."

She took a sip of her coffee. "Since you're insisting on that, I'll need to hear more about you, too, then."

Oliver stared out into the night, wondering how much she already knew since he'd had to disclose his involvement with Madison to Ava's superiors. "Okay, but you might not like what you hear."

THREE

Ava's heart hadn't jumped this much since basic training. She'd heard enough to be cautious, of course.

Oliver Davison had been around off and on for months now and he'd barely noticed Ava, so why did she suddenly have strange currents moving through her system each time he looked at her? Probably because today, he'd focused on her and implied she'd failed. But then, he'd failed, too. And he'd lost someone he loved through a brutal murder. The team had been briefed about him before he ever arrived. His fiancée, Madison Ackler, had been the Red Rose Killer's first victim. Ava didn't know if that was a coincidence or there was a history there, but she wasn't going to grill the man on it. She did know that Madison Ackler and Boyd Sullivan had gone to high school together.

She had to remember that and try to be kind about things. But while she felt sympathy for his loss, she still had a job to do. Or maybe she was tense around him because she'd lost someone she loved, too, and they had that in common.

Stop making excuses.

They had been forced together but in the worst kind of way. Over death and a missing child and an evil, sick man who wouldn't stop until they caught him. But that didn't make her ready to share her past or her other failures with Oliver Davison. She didn't want him to do an FBI analysis on her either.

"Hey, are you okay?" he asked, true concern in the question.

"I will be," she replied. And then to hide all the emotions boiling up inside of her, she tore into her burger. Stress eating to the rescue.

It had been a long, tough day and he'd gotten in her way and gotten *to* her. That wouldn't happen again. Dealing with an intense, dogged FBI agent one-on-one was different from watching him across the room. Not that she'd done that. Okay, maybe once or twice. And he must have noticed her, too, since he knew she guzzled coffee like a brewing machine.

But enough of that for now.

"Tomorrow, I go back to the spot Roscoe alerted on and we dig some more. Roscoe is never wrong, so there's something there we're missing. I hope whatever was buried there didn't get washed away. And, Agent Davison, I really need you to stay out of my way."

"I was in your way today?"

Yes, you with your green eyes and that messy hair and your black working T-shirt. You have those sad eyes and that bad attitude. Yes, you.

"You held me up with your repeated, pointed questions."

"Part of my job."

"Don't do it again. And please stop using that excuse."

He grinned and dipped a french fry into a glob of ketchup. "I'll take the west end of the woods and you can take the east."

"Agreed." Then she took a sip of the water the waitress

had also brought and wondered if the air-conditioning had conked out. "I'm concerned that Sullivan might have the boy. He could have easily killed me today, but he didn't. Someone shot at me, though. I don't know if that someone was with him or after him, but I'm thinking with him because that makes more sense to me."

"And protecting him from you as you suspected," Oliver replied. "They could use the boy as leverage for an escape."

"I've already considered that, but why didn't they do that today?"

"Exactly, which is why I questioned you so heavily earlier," he said, his tone apologetic now. "We have to consider every angle. You know how it goes with serial killers."

"No, I don't know how it goes, but when I saw him today I certainly understood the horror of what he's done. I could have easily died out there and he would have gotten away with murder again. I hope we find him so I can ask him why he let me live."

"I'd like to ask him a few things, too."

Ava felt that tug again. Her heartstrings were getting a workout today. "I'm sure we'll have to stand in line," she replied, trying to stay on topic.

"Maybe you just showed up at the wrong time, surprised him and caught him off guard. Or maybe he knew you had a detail on you and he'd be shot dead if he did try to kill you."

"Buster was right there, but he didn't get in a shot because everything happened so fast."

"You said it yourself. Buster's being there along with Roscoe helped to save you." Oliver dipped another fry. "And the shooter saved Boyd Sullivan. It makes sense he's had a willing accomplice all this time."

"I don't know what to think," Ava admitted. "Turner Johnson's parents are so distraught and angry right now, it's hard to watch. And I get that. First, the kid goes missing from his yard and now they find out a dangerous serial killer is out in those woods, too. Then a storm hits. I can't imagine that kind of fear."

Oliver drained his coffee, his brow furrowed in frustration. "We have to hope he's found shelter, at least."

"I have another concern to consider, too," she said. "Those missing dogs Sullivan let out of the training center that night when he killed two of my coworkers. Some of the dogs still missing suffer severe PTSD and they could be roaming those woods. If Turner Johnson happens to come upon one of them, he could get hurt."

"You need to be careful on all fronts," Oliver said, his eyes holding concern again. "You got off easy today, Airman Esposito. But I have a gut feeling the Red Rose Killer is not done with you yet."

"Call me Ava," she said. "Since you're trying to scare me to death and all, I feel as if we're bonding."

"Call me Oliver, since I can thank you for the heartburn I'm surely going to have later," he replied, his expression wry. "I'm not trying to scare you. After watching you in action today, I don't think you can be rattled. And *that* scares *me*. Sullivan's a dangerous man."

From the way Oliver said that, she was reminded of how personal this had become for him. After all, he had a very good reason to hunt down Boyd Sullivan.

But she wasn't going to pry into the horror of that reason. She just prayed they'd both find what they were looking for.

"Okay, Roscoe, let's do this again," Ava said after Oliver had walked with her and Buster back to the marked spot the next morning. Word from the night shift wasn't good. There'd been no sign of the boy or the Red Rose Killer and no alerts from the K-9s. But they'd found several fresh campsites and patches of spent shells.

"Some from our weapons and some from whoever was shooting at you with an M4 rifle," Oliver reported. "Whoever it is, thankfully, they aren't a very good shot."

The storm had passed but it had left a lot of broken limbs and washed-over bramble in its path. Ava accepted that they wouldn't get very far today, but determination kept her from giving up. The sun was shining today, though, and even at seven in the morning, the late summer heat promised to be scalding hot.

Leaving his official SUV up on the muddy road into this area, Oliver gave instructions to a team that had arrived in another vehicle and brought off-road vehicles with them to continue the search. Then he and Ava trekked through the woods to begin another grueling day. But he'd told Ava he wanted to check around this spot again, too, since Sullivan had been in the area.

Oliver walked around the area by the cave, watching as Roscoe took up right where he'd left off after Ava had let him sniff the miniature toy and the boy's cap she'd brought back with them again today.

"Find," she told the Labrador.

Roscoe started digging again in the same spot near the entrance of the tiny cave.

Oliver hovered off to the side, doing his own search. They really hadn't shared anything much about each other last night. Ava had realized he was good at his job and determined to find Boyd Sullivan. Now she wanted to know more about him, which shouldn't be front and center on her mind today. But that sadness that shadowed him had clutched her heart.

"I thought you were leaving," she said when Oliver finished his search and came back to stand with her. "Did you find anything?"

Oliver gave her a questioning stare. "I am leaving, and no, I didn't find anything."

He looked as if he wanted to say more, but instead he nodded and turned to catch up with the team that today included Master Sergeant Westley James, Office of Special Investigations Special Officer Ian Steffen, Security Forces Captain Justin Blackwood and several others who worked with the SF, OSI or the Military Working Dog program.

Everyone wanted to capture Boyd Sullivan. But she knew they were all concerned about the boy, too.

Focusing on Roscoe and armed with a small handheld shovel, Ava bent to help dig. Yesterday, she'd allowed Roscoe to sniff the toy and baseball cap that belonged to Turner Johnson and she'd done the same again today, praying the rain hadn't washed away the scent Roscoe had picked up then.

"Hey, be careful," Oliver said before heading out.

Ava called him back. "Oliver, hold on."

He came hurrying back, his serviceable boots kicking up mud. "Yeah?"

"Chad Watson and his partner, Custer, did find one thing yesterday. A Buff."

He looked confused. "Buff?"

"A stretchy headband-type head cover. Dark navy and floral. Chad turned it over to the crime lab."

Oliver took off his dark shades and squinted. "Possibly belonging to a woman?"

"Possibly."

"Interesting. Thanks—I'll check with Forensics later." Then he gave her a smile and put his shades back on. "Talk to you soon."

Ava ignored the warm rush of comfort that encased her and instead watched where Roscoe kept pawing away in a spot near a small rock anchored beside the entrance of the cave.

Buster stood a few feet away with his rifle held near his chest, ever vigilant. He'd been a linebacker in college, and he was six feet of solid wall with a teddy bear's heart. But fierce when it came to protecting his colleagues and his country.

"What is it?" she asked Roscoe, knowing he'd do his best to show her. Ava did another scan of the rocks and mud.

Then she saw a tiny spot of red poking out of the wet dirt. Getting on her knees, she immediately praised Roscoe. "Good find. Way to go!"

After telling him to stay, she took her shovel and managed to dig around what looked like a small toy similar to the one Turner's parents had given her yesterday.

"Got it," she said, clearing the last of the mud away so she could lift the toy out. Wedged between the small rock and the outside wall of the cave, the toy had become jammed in a corner instead of washing away along with the dirt that had covered it before. A little red-and-white robot with big black eyes and a tiny black nylon cape. A small duct-taped label was hidden underneath the cape. And the name Turner Johnson was marked across it in permanent black ink.

Roscoe woofed his approval. The plastic and the material could contain oils and epidermis particles from the boy's hands, some of which would be buried in the grooves and seams inside the toy. The rock had protected the little robot from getting too wet. So had Turner Johnson lost this toy or had he been smart enough to hide it between the rock and the cave wall?

* * *

After calling in the find, Ava and Roscoe started out again. Roscoe seemed determined to go toward the west, so Ava made sure she alerted their path to everyone patrolling and searching the woods. They started tracking again in an area called the scent cone, which worked with the breezes, temperatures and humidity to carry a scent from the last known place the missing boy had been seen. Ava started at a higher elevation just past the first cave and worked down-wind from where the boy had disappeared, letting Roscoe move in a crisscross fashion back and forth through dirt, mud, rotting tree trunks, rocky terrain and dense foliage while she kept a vigilant watch for an ambush.

No one had been shot at today, so that was good. But it could also mean Sullivan had left and possibly taken the boy with him.

Even with the hot sun beaming through the pines and mesquite trees, there was a sinister darkness hanging over these woods. Remembering that Turner Johnson had been in his backyard, an area that should have been safe, Ava agreed with her superiors that now that Sullivan had been spotted, this area should be restricted until further notice. She moved toward the trail head in the more traf-ficked area, hoping that by going for the obvious she'd stumble on another piece of the puzzle.

It didn't take her long to come upon Oliver's team.

Buster grunted behind her and took out his canteen. "Mighty hot. Mighty hot."

"Yes, it is," she agreed, stopping to give Roscoe some water before she drank from her own rations.

Other members of their unit nodded and spoke and kept working. She wasn't sure anymore if they were look-ing for the child or the killer or both. Which scared her. What if they couldn't get to Turner in time?

"How you holding up?" Oliver said from behind her.

Ava whirled to greet him, noting his sweat-drenched T-shirt underneath his FBI-emblazoned bulletproof vest. "One small victory."

She showed him the toy robot she'd placed inside a paper evidence bag and stored in a pouch on her utility belt. "We reported our finding to his parents, but this doesn't mean he's still alive."

"Maybe the kid lost the toy, and he came looking for it and got lost himself," Oliver said, doing that frown-squint thing she'd noticed last night and earlier today."

"I know, and I'm wondering if he lost it or if Sullivan hid it to cover kidnapping the boy. But then, what do I know about seven-year-olds?"

"Same here," he replied, a shard of longing passing through his eyes. Maybe, like her, he hoped to have a family one day. No matter their jobs, searching for a lost child always brought out the best in people, but it also stirred up the worst of their emotions. But they'd both been trained to school such things.

"How long have you been trying to catch Boyd Sullivan?" she asked as they pushed through bramble and called out Turner Johnson's name over and over.

"Too long," he retorted in a concise manner.

When he didn't say more, she let it go. But then, they stopped to catch their breaths underneath some mushrooming oaks and cascading mountain laurels.

"I'll explain that to you another time," he said in a gravelly voice. "How did you come into the MWD program? I mean, after you didn't become a pilot."

She shook her head. "I'll tell you that another time, too."

"I'll hold you to that."

Ava nodded. "Well, for now, we keep going." Once again, she let Roscoe sniff Turner's toy and cap. "I'll stay close by since it's getting late, but I want Roscoe to search this area, too. Maybe he'll pick up on Sullivan's scent. He's been in on most of the prior searches so you might get a break."

"I could use one."

Ava noticed the dark fatigue around his eyes. He was a good-looking man and obviously, like her, he had to stay in shape for his job. But there was a sorrow around him, as if he were searching for something other than a vicious killer. Again, she wondered how long he'd been chasing after Boyd Sullivan. He'd been in on the first arrest from what she remembered in the early briefings. But she wondered how long he could keep this up, too. That kind of tenaciousness could wear a person down.

No time now to ponder but, later, maybe he'd open up to her as he'd said.

Which meant she'd have to do the same with him, of course.

Or research his background on her own.

After they drank some water and shared an energy bar and she fed Roscoe and gave him some play time, they went in opposite directions again.

Five minutes into this new search, Roscoe alerted on another dark indention in a hill covered with overgrowth. He whined and kept glancing back at her. Not his usual alert. Something wasn't right.

Ava stepped forward and stomped through heavy vines and dense shrubs until she came to the dark crevice. Using her rifle to push back the foliage, she decided this had to be another cave.

Roscoe wouldn't let it go so she called out. "Turner? Turner Johnson? Are you in there? I'm here to help you."

She heard movement inside. Ava reported the find

over the radio and before she could make her next move, Oliver was right there with her.

"It could be your boy or it could be Sullivan," he whispered, drawing his weapon. "Either way, we go in together."

Another bonding moment, she thought, still confused about how this man brought so many of her feelings out of hiding. But he was just doing his job. He wanted to be the one to capture Sullivan.

Time for her to do the same with whoever was inside that cave. She prayed it was the boy.

Help us now, Lord. Help us to find this child.

But they needed to capture the Red Rose Killer, too.

As Oliver had said, either way, they were in this thing together now.

FOUR

When they stepped into the jagged opening to the cave, Oliver heard a low growl.

Halting Roscoe, Ava turned to Oliver. "That's not a person. It's an animal."

Oliver watched as she slipped on her protective gloves. "What are you doing?"

"It might be one of the missing dogs, possibly one of the ones suffering PTSD. I'm going in to check."

"Can he harm you?"

"Yes, if he's hungry and scared. Will you radio Westley for me?"

"Of course," Oliver said, "but I'm not leaving you in this cave alone."

"Okay, make the call."

Ava turned to Roscoe while Oliver stood just outside the opening and radioed their location. He watched as she ordered the K-9 to stay. The dog glanced at the back of the cave, whimpered a protest but sank down to do as he was told.

"I think Roscoe senses that the other dog is a friendly," Ava told Oliver when he finished the call to Westley James. "His protective instincts tend to kick in when he sees another dog."

Ava started talking quietly to the animal. "I took a PTSD course once," she whispered to Oliver. "I'm going to use what I learned on the dog to calm him down."

Cataloging that, he decided he'd ask her about it when she was out of danger. Staying quiet, he stood watch and tried to stay out of her way. When this was over, they'd have a lot to talk about.

"Hey, buddy," she said as she sank down near the door of the cave.

Oliver could see the trembling dog's shadow, but she kept talking in gentle, soft tones. "Roscoe and I are your friends. We're here to help you. You'll get to go home to the base and your warm, clean kennel and get all kinds of love, treats and good meals and chew toys. And the help you need, too."

Ava's voice wobbled, and Oliver guessed she had to be thinking of Chief Master Sergeant Clint Lockwood and her airmen friends Landon Martelli and Tamara Peterson, all of whom had died at the hands of Boyd Sullivan. He had purposely let the dogs out that night so long ago to shake everyone up and traumatize the animals.

Oliver's bones burned with the need to find the Red Rose Killer and end his reign of terror. But right now, he had to stay here with Ava.

The dog whimpered and growled low, as if Ava's changing mood had rattled him. "It's okay. No one is ever going to hurt you again. You're a hero and we're going to make you well so you can become a strong Military Working Dog." She smiled. "I have a friend named Isaac who's looking for a dog like you. A dog named Beacon saved Isaac's life over in Afghanistan. But he's lost somewhere far away. Maybe you can cheer up my friend until he can locate Beacon. How about that?"

Something inside Oliver's heart crumbled. He wanted

to comfort both the hurting dog and the woman who seemed so strong but right now seemed so broken, too. But just like the dog, if he moved too fast with Ava, she'd balk. She'd bypassed flying helicopters to do this. Was that a conscious decision, or did something painful keep her from fulfilling that dream?

Maybe she was right where she should be. And then she answered his question with her words.

Talking to the dog again in a calming voice, she said, "You know, we have a family here. We take care of each other and pray for each other. We've all been praying for you, too."

Prayer. Oliver had become so far removed from the faith his parents had instilled in him, he felt out of place hearing her words. He'd turned back to God after Madison's death, but he needed to be more intentional with his faith. Now would be a good time to take up the habit of praying again. He needed help in all areas of his life to get through this case.

If this woman had a strong faith, perhaps she could be an example to him.

The dog, which looked to be one of the missing German shepherds, stopped growling but lowered on its haunches, its dark gaze on Ava and Roscoe. Oliver kept checking for Westley, holding his breath. He loved dogs. Who didn't? But seeing how Ava handled this one made him more appreciative of what the MWD team did on a daily basis.

Slowly and carefully, Ava dug into her meal supply and found a peanut-butter granola bar.

"I'm thinking you're hungry, aren't you?"

She glanced back to where Oliver leaned against the entrance of the cave, her eyes meeting his, a soft understanding and longing in their depths. Ava pivoted back to the dog, carefully opening the paper covering the bar.

But Oliver would never forget that backward glance. It told him she was gentle and caring underneath that air force bluff.

"How about a snack to tide you over?"

Breaking half of the long bar, she tossed it toward the dog. Crouching and moving on its haunches, the dog gobbled the food and inched closer.

"Hey, Westley's here," Oliver said in a low voice, his breath gushing out in relief. Why was he so worried that the animal would hurt her? She knew what she was doing, after all.

Ava slowly slid away from the trembling dark-furred dog. "I'm going to go now, okay? But I'm leaving you in the best possible hands. He's my boss, so make me look good by bragging on me, okay?"

She scooted back, her gaze on the dog. The scared animal didn't move, but Oliver saw the apprehension in its eyes. The traumatized animal didn't want Ava to go.

Oliver didn't want her to go away either. Which scared him way more than a dog attack.

When she reached Roscoe, she scooted near. "Sir, come on in."

Westley entered the cave and got down on the dog's level. While Ava gave him a quick whispered update, he kept staring at the dog. Then he nodded to Ava. "One of our four stars." Turning back to the scared animal, he said, "We've got this, okay. You're home, soldier, and you won't ever be scared again."

Ava called to Roscoe. "Come."

The Labrador stood but turned back to the other dog, emitting a soft whimper from his throat.

Westley let out a light chuckle. "Hear that? Roscoe says chin up."

Ava made her way out. Oliver waited with his hand out

to help her up. She stood on trembling legs and glanced up at him, unable to speak.

Her sweet gaze shattered him. "Hey, it's okay. The dog's safe now."

Nodding, she wiped her eyes, clearly embarrassed at the tears forming there. "But, Oliver, Boyd Sullivan did this. He sent these scared, scarred dogs out to fend for themselves. We have to find him and we have to keep looking for Turner Johnson. Because if he did this, I don't want to think about what he'd do to an innocent child."

Oliver reached out a hand and then dropped it, memories jarring him. "I feel the same way."

Then he touched her arm and looked into her eyes.

"We'll keep searching, I promise. I know firsthand what Boyd Sullivan is capable of doing. And I am not going to stop until I either put him behind bars or put a bullet in him."

"Well, Turner Johnson's parents aren't happy, and I don't blame them," Ava told Oliver an hour after they'd found the German shepherd in the cave. "But they've been waiting and wondering and I had to report back to them. Not to mention, those two base reporters, Heidi Jenks and John Robinson, are all over this and I keep telling them 'No comment.' Lieutenant General Hall will probably want to have a nice chat with me, too."

"With all of us," Oliver retorted, his expression as dark as the rain that hovered on the horizon. These pop-up storms weren't helping the situation. "You've done everything you can and you're still out here searching, so the base commander should cut you some slack." He glanced around, then lowered his voice. "I also expect that annoying Anonymous Blogger to have all the details, too. I'm wondering if that person is Sullivan's helper."

Ava had to wonder, too. For months now, someone on base had found a way to get all the details of the Red Rose Killer case and blast them online. They suspected Heidi Jenks, but Ava figured Heidi wouldn't risk her journalism career with an unsubstantiated blog full of false accusations.

"I hadn't even thought about that," she said, "but yes, we can expect some sort of cryptic, inaccurate report on that front, too."

The phone call earlier to where the Johnsons were waiting at a nearby staging site had broken Ava's heart. Turner's parents were distraught and exhausted. Their child was missing in the same area where a dangerous man had been seen, so yes, they were frightened, angry and beyond being reasonable. She'd be the same way in their position. Reporters were always hovering around, but lately they'd become even more annoying. Heidi and John both worked for the base paper, with John being the lead reporter on the Red Rose Killer case, but they were in a competition of sorts to get the scoop on the Boyd Sullivan story. But Heidi seemed the more reasonable of the two, at least. Ava figured the determined reporter was probably with Turner's parents right about now, getting their take on this turn of events.

"Well, regardless of reporters and vicious bloggers, we still have our work cut out for us. No sign of Turner Johnson or Boyd Sullivan." She did a check around them and added, "I'm so afraid that wherever they are, they might be together. But I can't bring myself to voice that to Turner's parents."

Oliver walked with her through the hot, damp woods, Roscoe back on the job just up ahead of them. "They're feeling guilty that the kid slipped away. But they're also terrified about Boyd Sullivan, too. Drew Golosky turned up dead, and we barely had time to warn anyone."

Ava watched the path ahead. "I just pray it's not too late."

"At least the base has closed down this area. It's off-limits until further notice," Oliver said, his tone solemn.

"He let me live," Ava said, her mind still reeling from the last couple of days' work. "Why do I get the feeling it's not over between us, however?"

"Because you saw him, saw that feral look in his eyes. He doesn't have much to lose right now."

"Well, I do," she said, moving ahead with Roscoe, her heart burning with the need for justice and her prayers centered on finding a lost little boy.

She was also moving away from Oliver. Somehow, they'd become too close. She didn't do close. She was single and single-minded. Work consumed most of her time, and that was good enough for her. Or at least it had been up until now. But today, he'd stood there in the cave with her and another current of awareness had sizzled between them. Like heat lightning, there but hard to understand.

In spite of the circumstances, this man whom she didn't want to like had become ingrained in her psyche. In the span of two days, they'd bonded in more ways than she'd ever bonded with anyone else. Well, maybe one other person.

Never one to rush things, Ava didn't like the confusing feelings coursing over her each time Oliver was around. And now she was thinking about the man even after she'd purposely tried to distance herself from him. No, she'd been impulsive and rash once before in the love department. Not again.

She'd served with the one man who might have taken her heart. Julian Benton had been the gunner on her crew. They'd become close but he'd died in that chopper crash and left her numb with fear and afraid of life. She and Julian had never had a chance to explore where their feelings might have taken them because protocol and war had kept them too busy to take that next step.

So she'd put love out of her mind and she'd almost walked away from the world that had given her a home and hope.

Until the Military Working Dog program had saved her by offering her a way back to justice and that hope.

Did she dare go that deep with another man?

No. Not yet.

"Hey, be careful," he said, catching up with her.

"I'm always careful," she retorted. "And so is the trained animal guiding me."

"Any alerts?"

"Not yet."

"What made you switch to the MWD program?"

Oh, he wanted her to talk now, when she'd just been giving herself a mental pep talk. Since she didn't have much of a choice, Ava replied, "A chopper crash."

He kept his eyes straight ahead, his dark shades hiding his secrets. "You were on the front lines?"

"Yes."

"And you don't want to talk about it?"

"No."

"But you survived."

"I did."

"Others didn't survive?"

"No, they died."

He didn't miss a beat. "You'll tell me later when we are clean and cool and sitting in a nice restaurant?"

"You wish."

"I do wish," he said, his tone steel edged, his voice low and husky.

"Maybe one day I'll tell you but...you might not like what you hear. Isn't that what you said to me?"

"Oh, so we're gonna play that game where we try to hold on to our secrets until the very last minute?"

"One of my favorite games."

Before he could say more, Roscoe alerted with a low growl. A sign of danger, not a frightened child.

Oliver held Ava's arm and put a finger to his lips.

"I know how this works," she whispered, drawing her own weapon. Then she gave Roscoe the signal to "Go."

The big dog moved through the underbrush and rocky hillside, still growling low.

A bullet whizzed past Ava. Another hit at Roscoe's feet.

"Come," Ava commanded, bringing Roscoe back. Ava caught a glimpse of a figure dressed in dark jogging pants and a matching hoodie holding a gun aimed toward her.

Roscoe growled low, causing the other person to halt and lift the weapon. Ava did the same, ready for a face-off.

And then Oliver was there, pushing her down, a hail of gunfire and bullets bursting out in a harsh echo through the woods.

Overhead, birds flushed out of hiding and the whole forest came alive with critters being scared away and people shouting off in the distance. The shooter pivoted and took off.

Oliver rose up to get another shot with his handgun but it hit a tree while the culprit sprinted into the thicket.

"Stay here," he told Ava as he took off through the woods, reporting through his radio.

Ava didn't intend to stay here. She needed to be in on this hunt. And he needed to remember she was trained for this. If he hadn't tackled her, she might have been able to get a clear shot.

Or she could have been killed, and Roscoe right along with her.

Moving on her hands and knees, she motioned Roscoe to do the same. Together they crouched through the woods, stopping to listen and search ahead.

Her heart hammering, her pulse on overdrive, Ava scanned the perimeter around her and kept Roscoe close.

Where was Oliver? And where was the shooter?

FIVE

Oliver saw the dark figure moving ahead in a zigzag fashion. His heart still pumped adrenaline through his bloodstream as he thought how close the shooter had come to taking out Ava and her partner.

He followed, tree limbs slapping at his face, nettles pricking his skin, a new sensation moving through his system. Fear.

Fear for Ava.

He'd become distracted by the odd feelings, but now he'd reel those feelings in and get back on track. His focus had always been finding the Red Rose Killer. But he couldn't do that if he kept losing the trail because his mind was on a woman he'd only had a few conversations with over the last day or so.

So he kept going, following, listening. Just as before, the shooter had given up and run away. But someone had Ava in their crosshairs and this wouldn't end until Oliver did his job. Was the shooter just a distraction, or some sort of bodyguard for Boyd Sullivan? Tall and slender—it could have been a woman, but with the bulky, dark clothes and dark shades, it'd been hard to tell.

Soon, he had Security Forces members and K-9 handlers all around him.

"Find anything?" Master Sergeant Caleb Streeter asked, his tone blunt and clear. Caleb had taken over as head of the K-9 training center for a while when Westley had been guarding Felicity. Now that Westley and Felicity were married and she no longer reported to Westley, he was back with the K-9 unit.

"No. Lost the shooter in that thicket about one hundred yards from here."

"We haven't located anyone either. They shoot and disappear. Odd."

Oliver nodded at Caleb, wondering if the K-9 handler doubted him. "I'm heading back to where I left Ava."

Caleb looked around. "I'll search some of the other areas where we found campsites earlier."

Winded and disappointed yet again, Oliver stopped and radioed to the rest of the team. "Lost contact north of staging area." He named the coordinates and turned to walk back to where he'd left Ava and Roscoe.

But when he got there, they were both gone.

Three hours later, Oliver had gone his own way after trying to call Ava's phone. She wasn't picking up. He knew she was okay. Caleb had come back around and informed Oliver that Ava and a couple of other handlers had gone off in another direction.

Without Oliver, apparently.

Was she feeling the same way about things between them?

Was that why she'd suddenly left him in the dust?

Sure, she was capable and competent, but he'd tried to help her and protect her. That was a big no-no, especially with a military woman. He knew that and yet, his instincts had shouted to him to do just that. Now, wanting to protect Ava seemed to be edging out everything else, even his keen need to find Boyd Sullivan.

Dusk was beginning to shadow the woods. Another day gone, and the boy was still out here somewhere, along with a serial killer and a trigger-happy, hooded interloper. Deciding he'd camp out in the woods tonight, Oliver grabbed Chad Watson and started to back out.

"We've searched every inch of these woods, Special Agent," Chad said. "Not a complaint, just an observation."

"Duly noted," Oliver replied in a clipped tone. "You have something better to do tonight?"

Chad grinned and guided Custer through the bramble. "Well, I did." He shrugged. "It wasn't going anywhere, anyway."

"Oh, so this is about a relationship with a woman," Oliver retorted, stomping harder against the slanted sun rays chasing them.

"Isn't that always the case?"

"I wouldn't know," Oliver retorted. "I'm always working."

Chad caught up with him, his eyes on the dark gold-and-black Malinois sniffing the ground and the air. "Well, you need to change that tactic. You know what they say about all work…"

"Yeah, I know," Oliver replied. "Makes for me finding a serial killer."

She was running out of daylight and time.

The longer Turner was out there, the worse off he'd become. Ava feared he couldn't take another long night. While the temperatures were warm, the bugs, snakes and other predators could do the boy in.

Or worse, the Red Rose Killer could be holding him.

But surely by now they would have heard Boyd Sullivan's demands if he'd decided to use the boy for collateral.

Was the mysterious shooter his decoy, a distraction so Boyd could keep moving? Sullivan knew how the military dogs and their handlers worked. He could erase any signs or scents of himself. He'd broken into their headquarters and let most of their dogs escape, so the man wasn't stupid. He'd planned this attack, and he was always one step ahead of them.

Following Roscoe on yet another back-and-forth grid, Ava decided if they ever found the little boy, she wouldn't come into these woods again. She'd find a river somewhere and sit and take in the fresh air and enjoy the sun shining down on her.

In here, traipsing around with so much at stake, she'd turned her turmoil into feelings for a man who'd hovered in her peripheral vision for months now. She didn't need that kind of weakness holding her back. From now on, she'd focus on her job and forget the way Oliver Davison made her feel.

But his arms around her protecting her earlier today— that would be hard to forget. Or the way his green eyes widened when he was concerned, or the way he smelled fresh and clean even when they were out in the heat and humidity. And especially, the way his gaze had held hers when she'd looked over her shoulder at him in that cave with the K-9. He'd seen her pain. And she was pretty sure he'd felt that kind of intense pain himself.

Another crack in her armor.

But did he truly see her or notice this connection between them?

He had to have. They'd felt something that had caused them to break apart, even with someone shooting at them.

"I need to get that out of my head," she mumbled, her

eyes on Roscoe. And yet she wasn't really doing her job to the max right now.

Because the next thing she knew, Roscoe took off and headed straight for the edge of a high bluff. And almost took Ava over the edge with him.

Oliver was about to call it a night when he received a call on his cell.

"Davison," he said, irritated and tired.

It was the lab. "Special Agent Davison, just wanted to report we didn't find any definitive DNA on the floral Buff your people found in the reserve behind Canyon Air Force Base."

Stomping the ground, Oliver gritted his teeth. "Okay, thank you."

Putting his phone away, he stared into the woods, wondering why he couldn't get a break on this case. And then he saw it. Just a slight opening to what looked like one of the many caves hiding in this vast reserve. And he was pretty sure he'd seen a light flaring inside.

He was headed that way when his cell buzzed again.

Glancing down, he saw Ava's number on the screen.

"Ava?" he said on a whisper, his eyes on the cave.

"I've found him, Oliver. I've found the little boy."

SIX

Ava stared down the steep incline, her heart flipping and pumping a too-fast beat. "Turner? Turner Johnson? I've come to help you, okay?"

She heard another whimper and caught sight of the little boy huddled up against the stone wall of an indention below. And then she heard something else. A yelp that sounded like a bark.

Looking down again, Ava was shocked to see a small black dog with the boy. Could it be one of the missing dogs from the kennels?

"I'm with the air force," she said, calling out again. "Search-and-Rescue. I have my K-9 partner, Roscoe, with me. He sniffed until he found you."

"I found a dog, too," Turner called out. "He stayed with me when the storm came."

The tiny figure shuffled and moved, the little dog hopping around him, and Ava's heart did another rapid thump. The indention where they were sheltered was narrow, only a foot or so wide, with craggy jagged rocks and sturdy saplings down below.

"Stay there. Don't move, okay? We'll come down to you. I've got lots of help on the way."

Roscoe woofed, and the young dog barked in reply. She

took a moment to do a visual check of the boy. He was dirty and had scratches and welts all over his arms and face, but he looked okay otherwise. Alive. He was alive.

And alone, except for his furry companion. Hoping the furry little mutt was one of their missing dogs, she blinked back tears.

"Do you and the dog get along okay?" she called, amazed that the dog and Turner had found each other.

"Yes, ma'am. He's sweet, and he kept me warm. I'm keeping him."

Ava had to smile at that firm retort. They'd have to see about that later, but it made sense to her.

"How'd you get down there?" Ava asked, to keep him occupied while she tried to find the best way to get to him. Could they bring in a chopper? Possibly, but if not, she'd have to get the team to help get him out.

"I didn't want the bad guy to hurt me," the boy said. "He and that woman grabbed me and made me hide with them. But…I ran away when they started fighting and this looked like a safe place. The dog followed me 'cause I fed him some of my rations."

"You brought rations?"

Turner looked guilty. "I was playing soldier, and I snuck out the fence. I had a couple of energy bars."

"That's good. That's smart even if you did disobey your parents," Ava said, the sound of motors roaring to life echoing over the woods. She'd tried to stay away from Oliver, but she sure wanted him here now. "The bad guy is gone. He won't hurt you again."

"Promise?" Another whimper that sounded like a sob. "'Cause he told me he'd throw me off the bluff and kill my mom and dad if I talked to anyone."

"My dog and I won't let him near you," Ava said, her

tone firm and edged with anger. "You're safe now. Are you hurt?"

"No. Just sore and tired. Got a scratched knee. I'm hungry, too. And Stormy's hungry. We ate the last of my snack bars."

Stormy? The dog, of course.

"Soon you'll be with your parents and we'll feed both of you," she said. "Now, stay still while I figure a way down."

"Are they mad?"

"No, but they are sure worried."

"There's a way," Turner said, pointing past her. "I found a path."

Seeing a narrow, jagged formation that did look like steps, she motioned Roscoe. "Go," she said, indicating the path. "Guard."

Roscoe sniffed the dirt and rocks and then carefully made his way down the winding slope.

Watching his every step, she called out, "Hey, Turner, I'm sending you my buddy. He's going to watch over you and Stormy, okay?"

The scared kid glanced up. "Will he bite me?"

"No. But do me a favor and don't pet him. He's working, so let him do his job. He's going to keep you company until I can get there." And she hoped little Stormy wouldn't try to get friendly with Roscoe. "And hold tight to Stormy."

"All right."

Ava heard what sounded like an off-road vehicle coming at them. Turning, she drew her weapon, but before the ATV stopped, Oliver was out and running toward her, Chad and Custer with him.

"Where?" he asked, his hand touching her arm.

"Down here. And I think he has one of our missing

dogs with him." She pointed to the overhang on the rocky bluff and then showed Oliver the treacherous rocks forming a path. "He said he'd taken that way down. I sent Roscoe down after him."

Oliver glanced back at Chad. "See if there's some rope in the ATV supply box." Then he turned to Ava. "I'm going down to get him. Cover me?"

"Cover you?" She glanced around. "Do you think they're watching?"

"Just trying to plan ahead," he said, adjusting the vest that identified him as FBI.

"I'm going down with you," she said.

He shook his head, but she held up a hand. "Look, Oliver, I've been searching for this boy for days now. I'm going down there because I told him I'm here to help him. And…it is my job."

Oliver gave her a look of admiration and frustration. "Okay, of course. I'm not trying to take over your case."

"We'll argue about this later," she said. "Let's go."

Chad came back with a coil of nylon rope. "Found this."

"Cover us," Oliver said. "And hold on to the rope in case we need some help coming up."

Chad looked down to where Turner sat with his knees held to his chest, Stormy right up against his trembling body.

"And make sure the paramedics know we're bringing him to the staging area," Ava said to Chad. "Call a chopper to medevac him to the hospital."

"Yes, ma'am." Chad threw his rifle strap over his shoulder and did as she asked, all the while watching the darkening woods, Custer at his side.

Oliver went first and Ava carefully followed, but one of her boots caught on a root and she slipped.

Right into Oliver's arms.

His gaze held hers as he righted her, but the awareness between them hit like a bolt of Texas-size lightning. "Hey, I got you."

"I'm good, thanks," she said, pulling away. Looking down, she thought how close she'd come to crashing through bramble and rocks to the gully below. Then she thanked God that Turner had made it to this secluded hiding place.

She was so glad Oliver had come, but now she wished she hadn't had that moment of weakness. After calling the proper people in the chain of command, she'd immediately called Oliver, too.

Why?

Because they'd been in this together since yesterday's rainy afternoon. He'd helped her, and she'd helped him. They'd worked to find the boy and Oliver had done so instead of rushing off to find Boyd Sullivan. He'd put his search on the line to help her.

Had he put his heart on the line, too?

So stop being so petty with him.

Feeling contrite, she took hold of his T-shirt sleeve.

Glancing over his shoulder, he gave her a soft smile. "Almost there."

Overhead, they heard the medical helicopter moving through the air.

Spotting Roscoe and the boy who sat with an arm curled around the scared puppy, Ava stepped onto the narrow ledge where the boy was perched. "Hey, Turner. I'm Ava. And this is Oliver. He's an FBI agent."

Turner's eyes widened. "Did you find the bad guy?"

Oliver shot a glance at Ava, then squatted in front of Turner. "Not yet. But we will. Did you see him?"

Turner rubbed a grimy hand across his nose and bobbed his head. "Yes, sir. I got far back in the woods and couldn't find the path home and I saw him and then he chased me. He and the woman made me go with them. The man said they'd have to kill me, but the woman didn't want to do that. She just wanted to keep me and scare me. They got real mad at each other and were screaming so I ran and found a cave and I hid my toy 'cause he was making fun of me and took one of my toys. I hid the other one so maybe somebody would find it."

Ava shuddered but got a grip on her emotions. "You were smart to hide your little robot. Roscoe and I found it, so we knew you were still lost out here."

Roscoe's ears lifted, but he kept his eyes on the boy he was ordered to guard.

Turner was wound up now, however, which only made the little black dog with him turn in circles and woof tiny barks. Ava managed to get the puppy calmed down with some treats she kept for Roscoe.

"How'd you get away?" Oliver asked, his tone conversational.

"The woman told him not to kill me 'cause I'm just a kid. She kept saying, 'Remember when you were a kid. Remember what happened.' They argued and I ran away and found another cave. Then the rain came and I had to stay there."

Oliver shot Ava a glance, then checked the dog with Turner. "How did you and this little fellow wind up here?"

"It was first light when they started screaming at each other again, so I saw the light outside of the cave and I shoved my toy behind that rock and I ran."

Turner gulped in air while Ava checked him all over for broken bones or any odd or swollen bites or marks, the excited puppy nipping at her hands and arms. "So you spent the night in the small cave with the bad people?"

"Yeah, but I found this place and then I heard people

talking and running through the woods. I had to keep Stormy quiet so they wouldn't find us."

"The bad people?" Oliver asked, looking around.

"Yeah. They sure like to fight." He shrugged and shivered all at the same time. "Me and Stormy heard voices, but I thought it was a trick. We stayed underneath the bluff. It hid us."

Oliver nodded his approval. "Sounds like you did everything right." Then he leaned close to Turner. "Listen, I'm gonna lift you up and try to get us to the top of the bluff. If we can't make it, we'll have someone else come and help, okay?"

"Okay," Turner replied, lifting his arms to Oliver's neck. "What about Stormy?"

"I've got Stormy," Ava said, scooping up the scrawny little dog that looked to be a mix between a poodle and terrier. Sneaking him another treat, she gave Roscoe an apologetic smile and turned back to Oliver and Turner.

Ava swallowed the lump in her throat. The boy looked so small in Oliver's big arms. Those same strong arms had held her close earlier, shielding her and grounding her.

"Let's go," Oliver said to Ava after he had Turner secure against his chest. "You and Roscoe go up first."

Turner glanced back at his hiding place. "I'm so glad Stormy found me."

"Me, too," Ava said, the little dog clinging to her uniform and sniffing her skin. "Stormy is safe now, too."

With darkness falling, they worked their way up the side of the bluff, rocks and dirt kicking out with each step they took. Oliver stopped midway and took a breath. "Almost there, Turner."

"I'm a scout," Turner explained. "I rationed the food in my backpack and looked for water and shelter. And I gave Stormy food so he'd like me."

"You are a trooper," Oliver said, his head close to the boy's. "I think you'll be promoted to Honorary FBI Special Agent."

Turner grinned at that.

Almost there.

Oliver had said that same thing to Ava earlier.

Thank You, God, for sending this man here to help all of us. And thank You for keeping Turner safe so we can return him to his family.

Oliver crested the last slippery chunk of rocks, gritting his teeth against the heat and the bugs. Dusk was hitting, and the mosquitoes were swarming in a mad dash to gnaw him to death.

Trying to shield Turner from any more bites, he grunted and stretched his leg to reach the summit of the tall bluff.

He made it up the last of the dangerous steps and handed the boy off to Chad so he could turn and help Ava while Roscoe moved ahead.

Chad sat Turner down on a rock and checked him over. "Hey, dude. You are one hard kid to find."

Turner bobbed his head. "Are you FBI or K-9?"

Chad chuckled and ruffled the boy's sweat-dampened hair. "I'm Chad, a member of the K-9 unit. And this is my partner, Custer."

"Another dog," Turner said, grinning. "I can't wait to tell Mom and Dad about Stormy."

"Stormy?" Chad mouthed over his head.

"Right here," Ava said, holding up the bundle of skinny black energy. "He wants to keep the puppy but we'll have to make sure he's clear to do so. This one was geared to become a service dog so…Turner might need him."

Chad nodded. "Ah, I see." Then he turned serious.

"Chopper is landing at the staging area, ma'am. We are to bring the kid by ATV, provided he's uninjured and able to travel."

Ava handed Turner some water and a granola bar. "He's fine, but he'll need to be checked over."

Chad knelt by Turner and did another thorough check. "I'm finding bones, lots of bones. And I see eyes. Two very brown eyes. And yep, he has a tongue and ears."

Turner giggled. "Are you a doctor?"

"Nah," Chad replied. "I'm just pretending to be one. But seriously, bro, do you hurt bad anywhere?"

"No," Turner said. "I itch, and I need a bath." Then his big eyes filled with moisture. "And I want my mom."

Chad gave him an eye-level stare. "We can handle that."

Ava mouthed a "Thank you" to Chad and decided she'd give him a commendation as soon as they were all safe back at base.

Then she held the puppy tight and turned to Oliver. "Thank you, too."

His gaze held hers. "For what?"

"For coming to our rescue."

"You had it," he said, waving off her thanks. "But I'm glad you called me." With a shrug, he added, "We're in this together, Ava."

They stood for a moment, no words being spoken. They didn't need to talk. This very important victory held them together now.

Chad stood. "I'll go get the—"

Shots rang out and Chad spun, grabbing his shoulder. "I'm hit," he said before crumbling to the ground.

Ava dived for Turner and Oliver fell with her, covering both of them as bullets flew by them, hitting trees and bushes.

"Roscoe, search," Ava called. Both Custer and Roscoe were barking and prancing.

Chad called out a weak command to Custer and both dogs took off in the direction of the shots.

"Follow them," Ava shouted to Oliver. "Go. We'll be fine. I'll radio for help."

Oliver gave her one last look and took off through the woods, crouching to avoid being shot.

"I want my dad," Turner said, crumbling now that he was safe and the shock and adrenaline were merging in his tired little body.

"I know," Ava said, holding him close while he sobbed. "Chad, can you hear me?"

"I'm okay, ma'am. Hurts like all fire, but it's a through and through." He sat up and held his hand to his arm. "Just a lot of blood."

Ava put her arms on Turner's shoulders. "I'm going over there to help Airman Chad, okay?" After the boy bobbed his head, she said, "You stay behind this rock and hold on to Stormy, got it?"

He nodded, tears streaming down his face. "Is Chad okay? Is the FBI agent gonna be all right?"

"Sure, Chad's good," she said, praying it so. "And the FBI agent can take care of himself. He's tough like you."

Turner held to the squirming dog. "I'm okay."

Ava crawled to where Chad sat by a tree and after digging through her knapsack, found some gauze and tape. "I'll patch you up."

Chad nodded and drank some of the water she offered him. Once she had him bandaged, she asked, "Can you walk?"

"Yes, I think so," he said, sitting up, his color returning. But when he tried to stand, he wobbled.

"Okay, you're going to stay here and guard Turner, all right?"

"I can do that," Chad said, his handgun next to him.

"Then I can track FBI Agent Davison and the K-9s. They won't listen to his commands."

Chad grunted and nodded. "Yes, ma'am."

Crawling back to Turner, she said, "Here's the deal. We have help on the way and you're going to be fine. Chad will take care of you and Stormy."

"What about you?"

"I'm going to find my friend and Roscoe and Custer."

"But the bad man is shooting at us."

"Yes, but I have to follow my partner."

Before she could get going, vehicles plowed up on them, lights shining in her eyes while the sun sank down behind her to the west. Ava held her gun secure, ready to shoot.

"Esposito?"

She recognized the voice. Nick Donovan. A K-9 handler and good friend.

"Here, Lieutenant," she called, glad to see he had his bloodhound Annie with him.

After that, everything became a blur as she explained the situation and turned Chad and Turner over to Nick and the two Security Forces officers with him.

"I have to go after Oliver Davison," she said, urgency in her words.

"Why? Where is he?" Nick asked, his dark hair wet with perspiration.

"He went after the shooters. And he has Roscoe and Custer with him."

"Go," Nick said, a look of understanding in his eyes.

Ava took off but turned and hurried back to Chad.

"Thank you." Then she hugged Turner. "I'll talk to you later, I promise."

Then she was off. Running and praying she'd find Oliver safe and sound.

When she heard angry barks up the path into the deep woods, Ava sprinted in that direction.

Another round of gunshots echoed like a death knell over the forest.

SEVEN

Oliver whirled when he heard footsteps behind him.

"Ava!"

"Sorry," she said, her weapon protecting her. "I didn't mean to sneak up on you, but I have to get to the dogs."

"Hear them?" Oliver said as he put his hand on her back and they both crouched low. "They've cornered someone."

She nodded. "They're doing the angry bark, which means they've sniffed out someone or something familiar but possibly hostile."

Oliver guided her into a dark copse of trees. "I was about to find them. But you're here now, so take over and do your thing. I'll back you up."

"I hear water running," she said, whirling past him and out into the open.

"Look, Oliver," she said, disappointment in her words.

Oliver saw the K-9s barking near a stream, their heads lifted to the woods beyond the water. "They lost the scent."

"Let's go see. They might have something, and if we can get across the water—"

She didn't wait on him, so Oliver took off behind Ava. They were met with a volley of rifle shots.

Ava called back the dogs and hit the dirt.

Oliver fell down beside her. "They'll shoot all of us and end this right here."

"We need reinforcements," Ava said, reaching for her cell.

But Oliver stopped her. "No. We are getting you back to base and we are letting the next shift take over."

"This is our case to handle, Oliver."

He shook his head. "No, Ava. You were here to find the boy and you did that. Now I take over and find Sullivan."

"I'm not letting this go," she retorted, her head inching up only to be greeted with more gunfire. "They've tried to shoot me so many times I've lost count and frankly, I'm tired of it."

Oliver knew it wouldn't be wise to argue with the woman. She had fire in her eyes.

"Ava, you need to rest."

"I've been on tougher missions. I'll be okay."

"Okay, all right." He stood, causing her to grab him and yank him back before another round of shots scattered around them.

Oliver fell on the ground. "You're right. This is getting pretty tedious. Whoever this is, they obviously like using us for target practice."

"Ready to go in?" she asked, rolling away to lift up with her gun blazing.

Oliver's heart fell to his feet till he realized the shooting had stopped, thankfully. Because this woman was way too determined for her own good. And for his blood pressure.

"They're gone," he said, tugging her back. "Ava, I've already called in my location. I'll report where we lost them and the next team can take over. Justin and Westley will send someone around the other way to this location."

She stared up at him, frustration coloring her dirty, sweaty face. "We found Turner," she whispered as the reality of it hit her.

"We did," he said, breaking all the rules by wiping his finger across the smudge of dirt on her right cheek. "You did."

Bobbing her head, she let out a breath and gazed at him, realization and longing in her wide eyes. He had to wonder how long she'd been forgetting to breathe. Then, finally, she said, "I need to check on him."

Oliver sat staring at her too long, not sure what to do with her. The woman held back tears the way a dam held back a river. But she needed to have a good cry.

This kind of work could either shut down your emotions or bring them to the breaking point. He figured Boyd Sullivan had become broken by a cruel father long before he joined the air force, but did that give him the right to kill innocent people?

And did that mean Oliver would be bitter and unhappy for the rest of his life because he couldn't bring the man to justice? His faith told him God would be the final judge for Boyd Sullivan. Maybe he should consider that and let others with a fresh approach step in.

Testing that theory, he said, "Good idea. Checking on Turner sounds way better than following yet another dead end."

"Why can't we find them, Oliver?" she said as they stood and started back. "A whole air force base and all of our Security Forces on the ground and we can't find Boyd Sullivan and this woman that Turner mentioned."

"I know, but Sullivan lives on the fringe of being a soldier. He knows all the rules and he breaks all of them. He has someone helping him on the inside because he's charismatic and savvy. Women are drawn to him because he has that whole bad-boy thing that they think they can fix. He uses them and he's using someone from this base to keep him alive."

"Wow. You've got the man pegged," she said, her tone calm now, understanding and acceptance in her eyes. "You must eat, sleep and breathe this stuff."

"I do," he admitted. But he couldn't bring himself to tell her how his gut churned with guilt and regret. And he sure didn't want Sullivan to hurt another woman because of him. Especially this woman. "But…"

"I know, just part of the job, right?"

He laughed at that, figuring she'd given him a moment of grace. "Let's get out of these hot, sticky woods and go have that dinner I promised," he said.

"That sounds good to me, but I'm supposed to be avoiding you."

"That works since I'm trying to avoid you, too."

She gave him a surprised appraisal. "So we just avoid each other together?"

"A perfect solution."

She glanced back behind them. "At least Sullivan hasn't killed anyone else. I guess that's something to be thankful for."

"The Anonymous Blogger has struck again."

Captain Justin Blackwood stared out over the conference room, his blue eyes full of fatigue. Those same eyes zoomed in on Ava.

They'd just attended a press conference where the captain and several others had been grilled, including Ava and Oliver who had rescued Turner Johnson.

And then Heidi Jenks had brought up the latest questions from the Anonymous Blogger. "Captain, any truth to the rumors that Security Forces and the FBI aren't getting along?"

Without even a blink, the captain had handled things. "We are working closely with Special Agent Oliver Davison, but make no mistake, the FBI understands this is our jurisdiction and we are all cooperating in order to find the Red Rose Killer."

"Maybe a little too much," another reporter shouted. "Seems the FBI agent and Senior Airman Ava Esposito have become very chummy."

Again, the captain maintained a steely control. "When you're together for days in the deep woods of the Hill Country, you tend to become fast friends." Shutting the cover on his electronic tablet, he said, "No further questions. Good day."

Once the reporters exited, the team stayed behind for reports and updates.

Oliver stood up behind Ava before the captain could begin. "I have nothing but respect for your team, Captain. I'm doing my job but I'm well aware of jurisdiction and protocol. Senior Airman Esposito and I have our differences, but we're working through them. The blogger is trying to make trouble where none exists."

Justin's astute gaze moved between Oliver and Ava. "The blogger either saw you two arguing and discussing or they've overheard speculation that you either hate each other a lot or like each other a little too much."

Ava whirled to Oliver, hoping he'd play along. "Did you plant that little tidbit to make me look bad?"

Looking surprised, he said, "Excuse me?"

Giving him a meaningful "don't blow this" stare, Ava went on. "We've worked closely all week and today, you helped me when I found Turner Johnson. We agreed we'd go visit him in the hospital after this meeting, right? So tell me you didn't go and leak anything to that misinformed, annoying blogger just because I was doing my job."

Oliver tried to look justifiably confused. "I don't know the blogger and I get along with just about everyone in this room. Even you, Airman Esposito. If you ask me, you're way overdue for that promotion to staff sergeant."

Turning back to the highly interested team members gathered around them, Oliver glanced around the room. "I think the blogger is connected to Boyd Sullivan somehow. The Red Rose Killer likes to stir the pot while he gets away from us. I suggest we focus on that and not idle, unsubstantiated gossip."

Captain Blackwood cleared his throat and held tight to the rare grin he was trying to hide. "Okay, then. I believe that clears that up. Now let's hear all the real reports. This is still a serious situation."

Then he glanced at Ava. "Good work today, Airman Esposito and Special Agent Davison. You two have put yourselves on the line way too much over the last few days so I think it's to be expected that someone could misinterpret your...er...discussions. But it concerns me how they're getting their facts. I'd hate to think someone within our ranks is passing confidential information."

"Thank you, sir," Ava replied, a blush coloring her face. "That concerns me, too."

Oliver nodded and breathed a sigh of relief. Then he went over every detail of the last few days, ending with where he and Ava had last heard shooting earlier tonight.

"We never saw the shooter, but the K-9s had them on the run. The shooter took to the stream, and the dogs lost the scent. Then they shot at the dogs and us."

"I've got people combing that area all night," the captain said. "They're moving deeper into the woods and we're advancing right along with them. Sullivan will be flushed out this time."

After they were dismissed, Oliver waited for Ava at the door. But when she turned to leave he heard the captain call her back.

"Esposito, a word please?"

Ava sent Oliver a concerned stare and then turned to face the always serious Captain Blackwood.

"Sir?" Ava waited, wondering if she was going to be called on the carpet for hanging out with Oliver Davison too much.

Justin took a breath and crossed his muscular arms over his chest. "You've had a rough week, Airman. I suggest you take the rest of the week off. Come back Monday, fresh and ready to go again."

"But, sir—"

"That was not a suggestion, Esposito. You came in contact with a serial killer and in spite of that, you made every effort to find that kid. I know your history. We don't need you relapsing into depression again the way you did after you were injured in that helicopter crash."

Ava lowered her head. "Sir, I'm fine. I haven't had any symptoms of PTSD since I joined the MWD program."

Justin dropped his hands to his side. "And I'd like to keep it that way. A few days of R & R can't hurt. Besides, Sullivan has you on his radar. He's had someone shooting at you even after he told you he wouldn't hurt you. He's sneaky and he'll strike back, sooner or later."

"So you want me to hide from Sullivan?"

"No. I want you to rest and stay aware."

"And to not be so high profile on this case right now?"

"That about sums it up, yes."

Ava nodded. "Yes, sir. Thank you."

But her insides churned with worry. She rarely took a day off. What would she do with a four-day leave?

When she left the conference room, Oliver stood waiting for her by the snack machine.

Then there was the problem of him, of course.

Four days of doing nothing would leave her with too much time to think about Oliver Davison.

"What was that all about?" Oliver asked, careful to keep his voice low since the whole team now had a scope on things that might or might not be happening with them.

Ava kept walking. "I just got four days leave."

"What? Why?"

"Orders, really," she said as she headed out the door from the training facility. "So I'm going home to get a shower and I'm changing into civilian clothes before we go to see Turner."

Oliver got that she wasn't ready to talk. "Okay, I'll do the same and…pick you up at your place?"

She whirled to her SUV. "Maybe we should meet at the hospital."

"If that's what you want?"

She held a hand to the driver's-side door. "I don't know what I want. I feel as if I'm being punished, but Captain Blackwood said it was out of concern for me. That I needed to rest and go low profile for a few days."

"That makes sense because of all the attempts on your life. No one else has been threatened, you realize? The shooter is definitely targeting you."

"Yes, and you, too. I also realize that this person doesn't intend to kill me or you. Whoever it is, they are a decoy so Sullivan can move farther into the woods."

Oliver saw the frustration in her expression. "A few days off might do you good."

"I doubt that. I'll start climbing the walls. But the captain was pretty clear. I don't have a choice."

"Shower, we'll visit Turner and then I'm treating you to dinner."

"People are already talking, Oliver. The blogger must have overheard someone discussing how we operate together. Or don't operate together."

"Let them talk. We have to eat."

She opened the SUV door. "Okay, but I'm taking Roscoe so there will be no doubt that even off duty, this is only a work meeting. He can sniff out any lurkers at the hospital."

"He'll be a big help," Oliver said, wanting to reach out to her. But he held back. "I'll pick you up in forty-five minutes."

"Do you know my address?"

"Of course."

"Of course," she echoed. "Just part of the job, right?"

"No. I wanted to know where to pick you up for our first date."

She shook her head. "This is not a date, Special Agent. I want to make that perfectly clear."

"As clear as mud," he replied.

Oliver watched her drive away, worried that she was going home to an empty house. But she lived on the same street as several of the other team members. They looked out for each other, though Ava would spit nails if he tried to protect her. Still, he hurried to his car and went back to the base hotel to get cleaned up.

He'd be at her house soon enough.

EIGHT

Ava heard a knock at her door and checked the peephole to be safe, Roscoe by her side. She'd gotten used to having Roscoe here and she didn't like feeling vulnerable.

But her fears were put to rest when she squinted through the tiny glass circle.

Oliver, and right on time.

She took a last look at the white cotton button-down shirt and capri jeans she'd dragged out of her closet to throw on with some bright pink sandals. Too much?

Not one to be fussy about her clothes, she smiled at the sandals. They were a birthday gift from her mom earlier this year, with a note that said, "Live bright, honey."

Her mom loved florals and prints in bright colors.

Ava, not so much. Maybe because her dark red hair always clashed with anything bright. But she wore the sandals tonight to give her strength and to put her in downtime mode. Maybe she did need a few days' rest.

Taking a breath, she tossed her hair off her shoulders, threw on some earrings and opened the door to find Oliver standing there, looking way too good in a navy blue T-shirt and jeans.

"And boots," she said, not even realizing she'd spoken out loud. "You wore your boots."

"For you," he replied, stepping inside and lifting a foot to reveal what looked like hand-tooled rich brown cowboy boots. "You live close to Boyd Sullivan's half sister, Zoe."

Ava reached for her purse, used to his blunt switches in conversation. "Yes, but she's married now. She's Zoe Colson. I barely knew her before. Now we chat a lot in passing. She kept to herself until Linc Colson came along. They had a quick ceremony in their uniforms, performed by Pastor Harmon, from what Zoe told Felicity and me— and they're happy together. I visit with them now and then. I feel sorry for her since everyone suspected her of helping her brother."

A few months ago, Linc Colson, a tech sergeant and Security Forces investigator, had become Zoe Sullivan's bodyguard after she'd been targeted by Michael Orleck, a man who'd failed her training class. Zoe, a staff sergeant and flight instructor, had been the victim of his "gaslighting" pranks. He hoped to make it look like Zoe was having a breakdown because of her half brother Boyd and his killing sprees. But Linc helped her figure things out, and Orleck and a female accomplice were apprehended.

Since Oliver knew all of this, she said, "Zoe can't help that Boyd is her half brother."

Oliver lifted his chin. "Well, we've cleared her. She has had no contact with Boyd since he escaped."

"Yes, so why that concerned look on your face?"

"Just going over the angles. He could still try to get to you through her."

"Zoe wouldn't allow that," Ava said, glancing around her tiny but tidy apartment located on Base Boulevard,

Rescue Operation

where a lot of people she knew lived. "Besides, Sullivan had his chance with me in the woods—several times if I count his accomplice shooting at me. I'm sure he's moving on, and he could be miles away by now."

Oliver didn't look so sure, but he didn't pester her about it. Instead, he did a standard FBI sweep of the living room and kitchen and then stared down the short hallway to the bath and bedroom.

Her one-bedroom apartment was a single story, with a small front porch and an open patio and small backyard that opened to the common area and some woods behind. She used the place for sleeping and eating and watching sappy movies.

But now she wished it looked a little more like a home since Oliver's astute gaze had scanned the place. Was he still worried about her safety? Or checking out her sad lifestyle?

"Everything seemed okay when you got home?" he asked, confirming the answer to her question.

So maybe he didn't care about the dead plant on the table and the dust on the windowsills.

"Yes. Just stifling hot. I turned the air down so I can sleep better tonight."

"I'm glad you have Roscoe with you."

"Me, too. It'll be tough to let him go back to the kennels after this."

Oliver nodded at Roscoe. "You're a keeper." Roscoe woofed a thank-you. Oliver laughed and escorted her out, then scanned the street both ways. Seemingly satisfied after she'd put Roscoe in his kennel in the back, he opened the door to her SUV for her like a real gentleman.

Ava didn't have the heart to fuss at him for holding the door open for her. His chivalry was kind of endearing, but she didn't want to get used to it. Her work was done for a while, anyway. She'd still be part of the team searching for Sullivan, but she'd have to keep her distance from Oliver from now on.

At this dinner they needed to wrap things up and then take a step back.

Soon, they were at the base hospital, where Turner was spending the night as a precaution. The boy had been questioned by several members of the team searching for the Red Rose Killer, and Oliver had filled her in on the way over.

"He says he saw a woman and heard a woman and a man arguing about whether to kill him, but that the woman was dressed all in black, 'like a Ninja,' he says. Turner was so afraid, he wouldn't answer to anyone who called out his name."

But he'd answered to Ava, maybe because Roscoe had been with her or maybe because he didn't want to spend another night in the woods, huddling on a ledge.

After Turner's parents had thanked both of them, Ava and Oliver went into the little boy's room. Turner was sitting up in bed playing with his toys and watching an animated movie.

"Hey," he said with a grin, his bites looking clean and doctored and his scratches still evident but not as nasty looking. "You brought Roscoe?"

"Sure," Ava replied, smiling down at the boy. Roscoe woofed hello. "We just wanted to check on you."

"I'm fine," Turner said, his snaggletoothed grin doing Ava in. Since when had she thought of having her own little Cub Scout?

Since the fresh-and-clean-smelling man standing beside her had burst onto the scene.

After a few specific questions, Oliver made a big deal of calling Turner's parents back in so he could honor Turner with a plastic FBI badge. When both the agent and the little boy shot her dazzling smiles, Ava knew she was a goner.

She had to take four days away from this man, if nothing else.

They decided to have dinner at Carmen's. The Italian restaurant was intimate and quiet, with small tables covered in pretty checkered cloths and soft instrumental music playing in the background.

After the waitress put them in a back corner where Ava could keep Roscoe away from the comings and goings, Ava breathed a sigh of relief.

She could see the front door from here. Not that she worried about gossip. The base grapevine was common no matter where a person was stationed, since most military bases were like a city within a city and everyone knew everyone else.

But she did worry about the blogger, who seemed to thrive on making Security Forces, and especially the K-9 team, look bad. Why would anyone want to do that? Why stir up trouble where there wasn't any? Well, she and Oliver had grown close, but they were both toeing the line on their feelings. They'd spent the better part of their time together in the reserve behind the base, so the person had to be connected to Boyd Sullivan in some way to have even seen them together.

Unless the blogger was a member of the team?

She didn't even want to think about that.

"The scents coming out of that kitchen smell really good," Oliver said, his gaze on her instead of the menu. "Hey, are you okay with this?"

"With what?" she asked, coming out of her stupor. "Yes, I love Carmen's. The lasagna is so good. My favorite."

"No, I mean…this…us, together in public."

Ava put down her menu and stared at the artificial daisies in the center of the table. "I don't care what people think and I can't control gossip, but I wish we could figure out who the blogger is. Do you think it's Sullivan?"

"Only if he has a really good Wi-Fi signal from the woods."

"Could it be someone on the inside?"

"You mean from Security Forces?"

"I don't know. I'm just trying to figure how the blogger's reports always seem so close to the truth."

"Yeah, they nailed us. Arguing one minute and… having dinner the next."

Shaking her head, she glanced around. "It could be anyone."

"Yes, but I think it's possibly someone from Sullivan's camp, not ours," Oliver replied, his tone firm.

"So you think it could be his female helper who loves to use us for target practice?"

"Could be. Another smoke screen to distract us from him. But he hasn't made a move this time around. We've confirmed through DNA and fingerprints that he killed Drew Golosky, but he hasn't killed since then, that we know of."

"Maybe he's bored and sent his accomplice to mess with us just to get some kicks, since that person seems to be the shooter."

"About the accomplice, the floral headband thing we found didn't pan out. No DNA, but the rain probably took care of that."

"Turner said he saw two people, a man and a woman. That confirms that the shooter could be a female."

"According to the report from Caleb Streeter, the boy described the man as looking exactly like Boyd Sullivan.

You saw Sullivan, so we know he's back, but you didn't see the person with him."

"And Turner didn't get a good look at the woman."

"He saw her but, like he said, she was heavily clothed and disguised. We'd need to do a lineup of anyone we suspect and let him pick one out."

"Is that wise?" Ava asked after the waitress took their orders. "He's just a little boy."

"It's the only choice we have right now."

Ava knew he was right, but Turner had been through the wringer out there all alone. The boy seemed okay, but the hospital had brought in therapists to make sure he'd recover emotionally, too.

The waitress brought their salads and lasagna, then placed some bread and butter on the table. "Eat up."

"Let's enjoy our food," Oliver suggested. "And then we'll go over the list of female suspects we know of."

"There could be others?"

"With Sullivan, that's a distinct possibility."

He looked as if he wanted to say more, but he held back. Instead, he took a drink of the mint iced tea they'd both ordered and grinned at her. "Go ahead. I love watching you eat."

They both dug in and Ava had to admit, the lasagna hit the spot. "I didn't realize how famished I was."

"Dessert?" he offered when the waitress cleared his empty plate and put the other half of Ava's lasagna in a to-go box.

"No, just some coffee," she told the smiling woman.

Once they had their coffee, Oliver settled back to stare at her again. "We've only really known each other a couple days," he pointed out. "Seems longer."

"Tired of me already, Special Agent?"

He looked at her—really looked at her. His gaze moved over her face, her lips, her hair, the silver feather earrings she'd put on at the last minute.

"I don't think I could ever get tired of you, Ava."

"You don't know me, really," she said to deflect the warmth spreading throughout her system. She couldn't do this. Not with him. He was too much to take in, to absorb, to understand. And what if he got hurt or killed? She'd have to go through that kind of anguish all over again.

He let out a rough sigh. "I'd like to know you, the good you and the bad you. All of you. And I have to tell you, Ava, I'm not one to be rash or impulsive. I calculate and plan and analyze. That's what I do. That's my job."

He stopped and looked down at his fingers cupped on the table. "My job has taken over my life. It's all I've had for years now, and that was fine until one day in April when you walked into the conference room and…something changed. I didn't even know it had changed until we ran up on each other in the woods."

April. That's when she'd first noticed him, too. So he had been watching her, and she had to admit she'd been keenly aware of him even if she had tried to deny that to herself over and over.

But that didn't mean anything. Or it could mean everything.

Trying hard to breathe, she bobbed her head and pushed at her hair. "Yes, Oliver, in the woods with a serial killer watching our every move. A man who kills for the pleasure of killing. You came here for him, right? You came here on a mission and my gut tells me you'll finish that mission, no matter what. No matter the cost."

Sitting up straight, she pushed back her chair. "It's a cost I'm not willing to pay. Not again."

* * *

Oliver grabbed her leftovers, threw some bills on the table to cover the meal and the tip, and hurried after Ava.

"I'm sorry," he said once they were outside. "I told you I don't do this sort of thing and I'm not about to cross that line now, not with so much at stake."

Why had he told her he'd like to know her better? Now she was running away faster than a fighter pilot doing a downward spiral. She'd just admitted she didn't want to be hurt again. Now he had to know what had happened and who had hurt her.

"It's okay," she said, waiting for Roscoe to hop into his kennel. "We've only known each other a short time and yes, it would be nice to become friends. But now I have four days off and I don't want to think about you or the woods or Boyd Sullivan."

Oliver put her food in the back seat, got in the vehicle and turned to her. "So does that mean you've *already* been thinking about me?"

Her eyes told him everything. Interested and aware, but afraid and fighting.

"I've been thinking about a lot of things," she admitted. "But I'm going to use this reprieve to regroup and remember why I'm here. I want to get to the next level. I'm ready and I've worked hard and—"

He stopped her protests with a finger to his lips. "Did you hear that?"

"What?" Ava went quiet and listened. She heard a car starting, a motor roaring to life.

"Go," Oliver said. "Hurry."

Ava backed up and peeled out of the parking lot, glad the base traffic was light. "What is it?"

"Someone was watching us," he said, his eyes on the

side mirror. "There." A black sedan pulled out and turned behind them.

Oliver's heart pumped a rapid beat. "They were sitting in the car. Must have been waiting for us to come out of the restaurant."

Ava glanced into the rearview mirror. "So you think because someone else started their car and idled the motor, they were spying on us?"

"No, I think they were planning to either run us down or follow us." He checked behind them. "And now they are following us."

Ava checked the mirror. "That sedan is behind us but it's staying back."

"Don't go to your place yet," he said. "Turn toward the training center."

Ava didn't argue with him. She watched the approaching vehicle and then sped toward the K-9 compound. "Surely they wouldn't follow us into the center?"

"We'll see. They got on base somehow."

They both watched as the car gained speed. But just as Ava put on her blinker and turned toward the center, a Security Forces SUV sat waiting at the turn-in to exit into traffic. The black car moved on by. The SF presence had scared them away.

"That was close," Oliver said.

"But we still can't be sure," Ava replied. "Better to think the worst and be cautious, right?"

"Right."

They remained silent while she circled back and took the road to her house.

Oliver's thoughts swirled in confusion as Ava parked the vehicle and they got out, Roscoe leading the way to the door. He'd find Boyd Sullivan and end this thing, but now he'd do it because he'd been assigned to find a killer. Because it was his job. He'd do it for Madison. He and Madison had dated and come close to getting married. No one could ever know that she'd betrayed him by going back to a man she'd briefly dated in high school.

Boyd Sullivan. The man who'd killed her because she was with Oliver.

No one needed to know, but maybe he should tell Ava, at least. So she'd understand about him. That he had no heart left to give to anyone again.

"Dinner was nice in spite of that creepy car following us," Ava said, her tone uncertain. "I guess I'll see you tomorrow."

Glancing past her, he said, "Since you insisted on coming back here, at least let me clear the rooms again for you."

"I know how to check my apartment, Oliver."

"Yes, but…I'd feel better. I'm not trying to be all macho. I just don't want to leave without knowing you're safe."

He looked up and down the street in front of the brick apartment building. "I don't see any suspicious cars, but I'd still like to check on things inside."

"Fine, come in and we'll check the rooms together."

Ava put the food on a small counter in the open kitchen. Flipping on lights, they cleared the living room and then headed down the hallway to the bath and bedroom. Roscoe stopped at the door and growled.

"Stay." Ava walked ahead of him into her bedroom and turned on the light.

And gasped.

"Oliver?"

Oliver moved past Roscoe and her to stare at the bed.

A red rose lay across the bright blue bedspread. And a note stood against a fluffy white pillow.

You saved the kid. Good for you. Now...I'm coming for you.

NINE

Ten minutes later, Ava's house was overflowing with crime-scene techs and K-9 handlers, Oliver right in the thick of things to make sure nothing from the crime scene was compromised.

She sat on the couch holding a glass of water someone had brought her, her mind whirling with the implications of what they'd found in her bedroom.

Boyd Sullivan had let her live long enough to save Turner Johnson.

But why, when according to Turner, the man they thought to be Sullivan had threatened to kill him?

What had the boy said—that the woman reminded the bad guy about something in his own childhood?

Turner's ability to recall key elements of their heated conversation could help solve that puzzle, at least. What had happened in Boyd Sullivan's childhood to make him so evil and yet, willing to let a child live and willing to let Ava live until she'd found the child?

Someone touched her on the arm.

Vanessa Gomez, second lieutenant and critical care nurse.

And one of the women suspected of being in cahoots with Boyd Sullivan. But how would Vanessa have time to go traipsing through the woods shooting people when she worked long hours at the base hospital?

"How you doing?" Vanessa asked Ava, her brown eyes full of what looked like genuine concern.

"I'm fine," Ava said. "But every time I get up to help, someone tells me to sit down and stay out of the way."

"They've got it under control," Vanessa said. "I had just gotten home and came over when I heard about what had happened."

Ava remembered Vanessa lived down the street from her.

"How did you hear?" Ava asked, suspicion her constant companion now.

"We have scanners at the hospital to report incoming and other things. My shift had just ended, so I asked to see you, since I've been looped in on this from the beginning."

Ava tried to calculate the distance from the hospital to her house. "Thanks for checking on me. I'm kind of jittery."

"Understandable," Vanessa said. She wore her long brown hair up in a haphazard messy bun. "You know, I'm a target, too. I got a rose back in April. I have a security guard escort me out of the hospital and some of the base patrols make sure I get home. And at home, I have K-9 Eagle assigned to me until further notice, and my brother, Aiden, lives there with me. I've been watching my back for months now and let me tell you, it's not any fun."

Ava's suspicions eased. She'd heard Vanessa's younger brother had come back from deployment with a serious case of PTSD. "I'm sure it's been awful and now that the Red Rose Killer is back, it's even worse."

"Yes." Vanessa glanced around at the activity. "He's

becoming bold again. We've heard he's hiding out in the woods. Quite a feat, you finding that little boy alive."

"Sullivan could have killed him."

"And you, too," Vanessa said. "Now you're on the list, so, Ava, take any precautions you can."

"I intend to," Ava answered. "But right now, I need something to do. I can't just sit here."

The front door opened and Roscoe came running in and galloped straight to her, Buster grinning behind him.

"Roscoe." She ruffled his golden fur and hugged him close. "I'm so glad you were here with me."

Her furry partner woofed his happiness, too. But Roscoe was a working dog. He lifted his head and started sniffing the air.

Oliver came in from the hallway. "I asked Buster to take him around back. They picked up a scent so we've got people combing the woods."

"He should go back over the apartment." Ava stood and ordered Roscoe down the hallway even though he'd cleared the apartment earlier. But he had alerted at her bedroom door. Oliver had rushed both of them away from the scene. Now she wanted answers. "Search."

Buster followed Oliver, along with a couple of techs and Captain Blackwood, all eager to see what else Roscoe might find. Ava thanked Vanessa for checking on her and hurried to the back of the apartment.

Roscoe stood with teeth bared and his fur standing straight up, same as he'd done earlier.

"He recognizes a scent," Oliver told her as he pulled her into the bedroom. "But we don't know who that scent belongs to."

Ava watched Roscoe, then grabbed some latex gloves and searched under her bed and all around the room. "I don't see anything out of the ordinary. And we know they came in through that window." She pointed to where they'd found a bent screen that someone had managed to put back on the window and a broken pane near the lock. "Roscoe alerted earlier and we didn't find anything else. He could be picking up a scent from someone in the house." She thought about Vanessa, but Roscoe had whizzed right past Vanessa.

Roscoe kept growling low, his fierce eyes on the window.

Oliver looked at Ava for a brief moment and then grabbed her and dived to the floor with her.

Just before a bullet pierced the wall behind where she'd been standing.

"I'm getting you out of here," Oliver said a few moments later, his body still shielding her.

Ava clung to him but tried to move away. "Oliver, I'm not going to run away scared."

He helped her sit up, and after he'd assured everyone she was all right, he leaned toward her, his dark head close to hers. "You should be scared, Ava. They're coming for you, one way or another, and sooner or later, they will get to you. Tonight was too close for comfort. They had a solid bead on you and we stopped them, but they won't miss next time."

"I'll be more careful," she said, her insides cold with dread, the sound of that kill shot still ringing in her ears.

How she'd do that, she wasn't sure. She'd tried to be cautious, but this entire week had been one big search and rescue. The adrenaline from that assignment had receded but now her heart rate was right back up. Out of worry for her safety.

And Oliver's.

Ava couldn't believe that whoever had broken in here had been hiding out, watching and waiting the whole time while a team of trained law enforcement officers and K-9s stormed her house and the woods. Had the car following them been a distraction so the killer could get in the house and then hide in the woods?

Oliver held her arm. "The minute you came into the bedroom, they tried to kill you. He's done toying with you. The boy is safe and now Sullivan needs a new kill. This has escalated beyond being careful."

"You're scaring me."

Captain Blackwood walked in and after salutes, he turned to Ava. "I agree with the special agent, Ava. You can't stay here alone."

"I'm taking her to San Antonio," Oliver said, his tone firm and sure.

"No," Ava said, shaking her head.

"Yes," the captain said, nodding his head. "Getting her off the base without him knowing is a good idea."

"Sir, with all due respect, you haven't sent any of the others off-site," Ava replied, thinking the last place she needed to be right now was with Oliver Davison.

"No, but they've all had protection and right now, I don't have anyone to spare. Oliver can still do his job at the FBI field office by searching for any loopholes we've missed and he can protect you, away from base, for the next four days, at least."

"But, sir—"

"That's not a suggestion, Airman. We'll clear the way and make sure we sneak you out of here so they can't find you."

"Yes, sir. If I go, Roscoe goes," she said, hoping they'd both agree.

"Might be risky," the captain replied. "Roscoe isn't used to the city. What do you think?"

She didn't want to leave her partner. "Because of his

breed and since he's SAR, he's more socially inclined than the hard-nosed bomb sniffers and terrorist hunters. I can handle him in crowds, sir. Besides, we probably won't venture out that much, if at all."

The captain gave her a curt nod. "Roscoe could use a break, too."

"It won't be that long," Oliver told her while she gathered some clothes. "I have a two-bedroom apartment and I'll give you all the space you need."

"What I need is my life back," she replied. "And you should be here, looking for Sullivan."

"I've got other agents scattered around and I had intended to report in and do some work from home this weekend anyway," he said. "You can help me go over the list of female suspects who might be helping Sullivan. I want to put them in that lineup I mentioned earlier."

Ava still didn't agree with that idea, but they might not have any other choice. If Turner could ID the woman, they could bring her in and question her. And maybe get a break.

"I'll help in any way I can since I'm being taken against my will."

They were alone in the room now, but the captain had stationed guards outside so they could sneak her out.

"Are you really going against your will?" Oliver asked her now, his tone soft and husky against her ear.

She couldn't answer that. Her heart wanted some time alone with this man but her head told her to sneak away from him and everyone else until she could figure this out.

"I'm going," she replied, stepping back. "That will have to be enough for now."

He nodded. "I'll take it because I'm not going to leave you alone here."

* * *

They set up a decoy—Special Agent Denise Logan, who'd been brought in not long ago to help with training one of the K-9s. Denise specialized in electronics and had worked with Senior Airman and training volunteer Chase McLear and a beagle named Queenie. Denise trained dogs in electronic detection but she was also good at surveillance and undercover work.

She'd been back on base this week to help with training again and to check on some of the missing Military Working Dogs and service dogs they'd found in the woods.

So, they brought her in disguised as a tech and then took Ava out, also disguised as the same tech.

Denise would stay in Ava's house with a trainee dog, hidden guards on the alert all around, in an effort to draw Sullivan or the shooter back to the house.

Normally, Oliver would have stayed close for such an operation, but right now he wanted Ava away from Canyon Air Force Base. And he wanted to start from scratch and go through the whole timeline to try to figure out how Boyd Sullivan's mind worked. The man was a naturalist and an extremist, so he knew how to hide in plain sight in those dense woods. He was rubbing their noses in it.

He wanted to toy with Oliver a little bit more, but Oliver wouldn't fall for his tricks any longer.

Oliver couldn't be everywhere and his priorities had now shifted to taking care of Ava first and leaving the hunt to the highly trained pros on the base.

Now with everything in place they were on their way to San Antonio, traveling in the dead of night with a detail behind them for an extra precaution.

"So it's about a thirty-minute drive to my place. It's downtown near the Riverwalk," Oliver told Ava.

"Fine."

She'd been quiet. Too quiet. Ava didn't like being handled. She was used to handling things all by herself.

"Tell me about your family," he said.

"You're trying to draw me out, Special Agent. And I don't want to talk to you right now."

Nope, not happy. She was using that special agent thing like a weapon.

"Are you going to pout for four days and waste the time we have together?"

"Yes."

"Ava, c'mon, we're all concerned about you. Sullivan veered off the beaten path to scare you, and he follows through on his threats."

"Yes, and several other people are on that list, too."

"Yes, but several are being protected around the clock and the others are being vigilant in staying safe."

"I can keep myself safe. Roscoe is with me twenty-four-seven these days. He saved me tonight. Well, you both saved me."

"Yes, and we're both here with you. I don't doubt your abilities, Ava, but someone tried to put a bullet in you last night while you were standing in your house."

When she didn't respond, he added, "Plus, your superior ordered some R & R for you since you've been in the woods for days now with very little rest and you were shot at on several different occasions while searching for Turner Johnson."

"What if they come after Turner?" she asked, her pout session forgotten now. "Maybe we should consider that instead of my safety."

"On it."

"You've got people protecting Turner?"

"We're watching his house. They already have a state-of-the-art security system. We haven't leaked anything that he told us to the press."

"Not even to Heidi?"

"No. Especially not to Heidi. You were at the press conference last night. We never mentioned that the boy had run into Boyd Sullivan."

"What if Turner tells someone?"

"I don't think he will. He's still scared, for one thing. And his parents are encouraging him to only talk to his doctors and therapists."

"But if he has to pick someone out of a lineup—"

"It will be done in secrecy."

She went back to pouting. He watched her shut down and lean toward the passenger-side door. Roscoe was tucked into the back, his head turning from left to right.

"Ava, I'm sorry. I can't help this need to protect you."

"And I can't help that it makes me angry. I'm not a shrinking violet, Oliver."

"I can tell," he said, trying to lighten things. "You're more of a fiery cactus flower. Pretty but prickly."

"Is that supposed to be a compliment?"

"Yes."

"Do you really think you can hide me in San Antonio?"

"It's a big city, and I know all the secret spots."

She was silent for a while and then shifted toward him. "Since we're stuck together, why don't you tell me about where you grew up?"

"Oh, so we're talking again?"

"No, I'm asking the questions now. I mean, I really don't even know you. You don't talk much about yourself, so now's your chance."

Oliver decided he'd try anything to draw her out and win her trust. Even talking about himself.

"I grew up in Yonkers, in a mostly Irish neighborhood. I thought my dad worked at a financial firm in New York City, but I found out when I was old enough to understand that he was FBI. He dealt with a lot of bad mafia people and put some of them away for a long time."

"So you followed in his footsteps?"

"Lived it and breathed it. Couldn't wait to get out of college and head to Quantico."

"How did your mother live with that? Both of you being FBI, I mean?"

Surprised at that question, he shook his head. "Not very well."

"Don't tell me he got killed while on duty?"

"No. He retired, and they moved to Florida."

She seemed to exhale after hearing that. "And your childhood?"

"Normal, fun, always running in packs with my diverse group of friends. I loved it."

"You really are too good to be true."

"You think that?"

"Why don't you tell me about what's really eating at you?"

"How do you know something is eating at me?"

"Because you get this sad look in your eyes at times, a look that I remember well. I used to see that same look each time I came upon a mirror."

"Did it go away?"

"It's getting better," she said, staring out over the highway.

"This person who died when you were in the chopper crash, was he special to you?"

"Yes."

Oliver swallowed and took a leap of faith. "I had someone special once. Or at least I thought she was special. But she lied to me and kind of ripped my heart out."

Ava didn't say a word. She waited.

Exiting the interstate, he drove a few more miles and then turned into a tree-lined street and made a left into an apartment complex. "The saddest part of it—I didn't really even love her."

TEN

Ava barely noticed the swanky gated community or the upstairs apartment that had a view of the entire city, including the nearby famous Riverwalk. The place was modern and minimalist with sleek lines and very little artwork or distractions.

But she didn't need a distraction in design. Stunned, she couldn't get past what he'd just said to her before they'd made their way up the elevator.

Oliver had been in love and he'd been betrayed? Was he referring to Madison Ackler?

But then, he hadn't really been in love?

She needed to know more about his relationship with the woman Boyd Sullivan had killed.

Much more.

"Are you hungry?" he asked, causing her to turn from the glass doors to the wide balcony.

"No. Just tired." Then she shrugged. "But I'm too wired to sleep just yet."

"You want answers."

"Of course I do. You might have tried leading with that 'I didn't love her' comment."

"I think my mom left some chamomile tea here last time they came to visit. I'll make you a cup."

"I hate hot tea." She moved across the wide, open room and sank down on a creamy leather couch by a cozy fireplace. "Stop with the patronizing. I want you to tell me the truth, Oliver. I assume you're talking about Madison, right?"

He let out a breath. "Yes, but there are things regarding this case that not many people know."

Ending the search for tea, he came and sat down on the couch then propped his booted feet on the glass coffee table.

"She and I met here in San Antonio about four years ago." Looking around, he shook his head. "She wanted it all because she came from a small Texas town. She wanted the city life and the night life and the good life."

"Did you try to give her all of that?" Ava asked, trying to picture him with that kind of woman.

"Yes, I did. But she tended to get bored easily. We lived near each other in downtown apartments and grew close pretty quickly. For a while, things were good. She worked as a paralegal with a prestigious firm and I did my job. We dated and I enjoyed her company. But Madison always held things back and she complained about my long hours."

"She hated your being FBI."

"How do you know that?"

"If she wanted it all and you had to give work your all, it doesn't add up, does it?"

Giving Ava an admiring stare, he finally said, "No."

"So she…started staying out with the girls, complaining that you never had time for her?"

"Did you know her?" he asked with a wry grin.

"No, but I know how it goes. I've seen a lot of that, being military. Anything to do with saving the world tends to take up a lot of time and energy."

"Yes, that is true. She wanted me to find a good desk job that paid more. Maybe something in the finance world."

"You'd last at that about two days, tops."

"You see, this is why we click, you and me."

They sat, eyes on each other, for a few heartbeats.

Ava blinked first. "Stop stalling and finish your story."

He cleared his throat, sat up and held his hands together. "Madison grew up in Dill, Texas. She went to high school with Boyd Sullivan. They dated briefly and went to the prom together…but Madison broke things off with him when he got too possessive after only a couple of dates."

Ava's stomach roiled while her pulse skidded to a stop. "So Boyd and Madison were close at one time and she ended it? Is that why he went back there and killed her?"

"Yes, that and the fact that she was with me."

He stood and moved to the fireplace to place a hand on the wooden mantel. "We were engaged."

Ava took in a breath and hurried to him to pull him around, her hand on his arm. "Wow. I don't remember all the details of the victims' backgrounds." Looking over at him, she asked, "How did she wind up dead back in Dill if she was living in San Antonio and engaged to you?"

"That's the rest of the story."

"Okay, I'm listening."

"He killed her first and then killed the other four. At first, I was a suspect, being the boyfriend. But I had a solid alibi. I was doing surveillance with another agent the night she was killed."

He took Ava's hands in his. "I had asked her to marry me, but I realized after I'd asked her that I wanted to get married for all the wrong reasons. Madison wanted children and a big house and the ideal suburban life. I cared about her and thought my image of a family man would be good for my job. Then I remembered what my mother had gone through and I…kind of balked on the marriage thing. When I tried to explain to Madison, we had a horrible fight and I broke up with her because I could see we'd never make it."

Holding tight to his hands, Ava asked, "So you tried to be honest with her, but things didn't work out?"

He closed his eyes and took another breath. "No, she got really angry and called me all kinds of names. Then she left. I thought she'd gone back to her apartment and that we could talk after she calmed down. Maybe we could just hold off on the wedding for a while to see if it was right. But when I didn't hear from her, a friend told me that Madison decided to go home to Dill for the weekend. But she didn't come back to the city that Sunday. I got the call late the next day, after searching for her everywhere. He shot her and left her inside her car on a rural road just outside of town. Left the final note on her body and then he killed all the others."

Ava swallowed the lump in her throat. Oliver's fiancée, gone in an instant. "Oliver…"

He held her hands but shook his head. "No, let me finish. I need to tell you all of it."

Ava nodded and waited, holding her breath for what might be next.

"After she died, a friend came to me and told me the truth. Madison went back to Dill, all right. And right into Boyd Sullivan's waiting arms."

Ava pulled away and stepped back, her gut burning. "They had kept in touch?"

"I think Sullivan was her first love but she couldn't deal with his dark side," Oliver said. "I think that sicko killed the woman he claimed he loved because he thought *she* loved me. I can't prove any of this, but I've put together enough bits and pieces to know they met back up somehow after she left Dill the first time and she had an affair with him. But she didn't want to break off things with me because she wanted me to be the man she married, while she kept him on the side. I believe he confronted her about me and she told him she wanted to marry me. The friend who told me all of this said Madison didn't want to acknowledge her love for Sullivan because he was a loose cannon and, in Madison's mind, a loser."

The puzzle started falling together in Ava's mind, too. "So he killed her when she threw you up to him?"

"I don't know. But knowing Madison, she might have blurted that out. She wanted the good life, which he couldn't give her."

Oliver's gaze met hers and she could see the torment of this horrible burden he'd been carrying. "He must have snapped when she turned him down again and then he wanted to get even with all of us. So…in a way, my being with Madison started this whole chain of events."

"No, Oliver, no. He's sick. He would have done this eventually anyway, and Madison obviously didn't love him, or you either, for that matter. She played both of you and that's not your fault. You can't think that way."

Oliver lifted his hands and then dropped them to his side. "But I have to think of all the angles, because I helped to put him away and he managed to escape. He's not done killing and he's targeting you now. I can't let him do this all over again."

Ava understood Oliver's intense need to protect her, but she worried he was going down a slippery slope.

Looking into her eyes, he said, "I'm the real target now. It's become personal between us. But he won't kill me, because that would be too easy. He'll go after the people I care about and that means you're high up on the list."

Ava digested that, her heart splitting, but she needed to

know a few other things, too. "Why haven't you told any of us this, Oliver? You're way too involved in this case."

"Because my SAC only offered me this opportunity if I'd stay focused on the whole case and not just Madison's murder. He picked me because I know the case, but he's watching me like a hawk, too. Trust me, I can't blow it again."

Pacing in front of the patio door, he turned to stare out at the city. "It's too late for me to help Madison. But I can't stand by and let this happen again. Not to you, Ava."

"He won't get to me."

"But he'll try. It's a matter of pride now. He has to win. I won't let him win again."

Ava wanted to pull him close, but that would be too tempting. He didn't need a romantic entanglement right now, and neither did she. She thought back over their time in that dense wilderness and how much the guilt must have been eating at him out there in the wild and each time he came home at night, knowing he'd let Sullivan get away yet again. No wonder he'd gone into hyper mode in trying to find the Red Rose Killer. Oliver had relived his fear and guilt when he'd seen that rose and note in her bedroom.

"I'm so sorry," she finally said. "Oliver, I'm sorry. We're going to find him, and maybe one day we'll understand why—what happened to make him so evil." Then she whispered, "But none of this is your fault. You have to keep telling yourself that."

Oliver looked at her, his gaze hungry for redemption as he stared into her eyes. "I've changed, Ava. After she died and I put together the truth, I took a long walk and wound up in a little church, and I prayed like I've never prayed before. I told the Lord I wanted to be a better man, a man who knew true love and felt things deeply, with all my soul."

"You are that man," she said, holding back tears. "Oliver, you are that man."

"I want to be," he said, his shoulders sagging. "But I keep slipping back into that old habit of doing my job and ignoring everything, including my faith. I want to bring in the Red Rose Killer, for Madison and for all the others he's killed. And now, for you."

Ava gave in and put her hands on his face and kissed him, her heart opening and accepting that something was happening between them. Something that went deeper than finding a killer.

"And for yourself," she whispered.

Oliver felt lighter, free, hopeful now. After he'd spilled the truth to her, Ava had softened. He knew she could be a good friend, if nothing else. Yes, she'd kissed him, but that only meant she had empathy for his situation. They'd discussed the case and life in general well into the dawn and finally, exhausted, he'd escorted her to her room. After making sure Roscoe was settled near her bed and the alarm was set and no suspicious cars or people were hanging around outside, Oliver had finally slept for a few hours.

Now they'd had coffee and bagels and were about to get busy with work. Roscoe sat obediently after his breakfast and a fast walk in the neighborhood doggie park, both Ava and Oliver careful that no one suspicious was around.

"In spite of the gruesome details," he said now, "I feel better having told you the truth. I've never told anyone the whole story."

"Not even your SAC?"

"Oh, he found out right away. Once I was cleared as a suspect, my SAC watched me like a hawk because I became obsessed with finding Madison's killer. Then when the reports about the other killings in Dill came in, I got sick to my stomach and worked day and night until my SAC pulled me off the case and told me to go home and sleep. But I couldn't sleep or eat or do much of anything. I went through the ordeal of packing up some more of her things and I found a note."

"A note?" Ava turned to him. "From Sullivan?"

"I believe so. A card with a dried red rose pressed inside. The note said, 'I'll find you again one day.'"

"That's the Red Rose Killer," Ava said. "He must have had it in for her after she dumped him in high school, but you had to connect him to the others, too."

"Exactly. So I explained my theory to my SAC and he got serious about things then, but he still wanted me off the case. Of course, we had a solid case when he went to trial. Madison must have had that note since high school. I don't know."

"So you thought it was over when he went to prison?"

"Yes, I tried to give up but I'd still wake up at night in a cold sweat, thinking about how she died. He was in prison by then and I thought I had justice for Madison. Then he escaped and killed again, and now I'm back on it because I know more about the man then most, but still not nearly enough. When Sullivan escaped, my SAC came to me and asked me if I could handle it."

"The case or the fact that Sullivan escaped?"

"Both. He offered me the case, provided I took things slow and had a lot of backup. He knew the base had jurisdiction but he allowed me to consult, so to speak, since I know this investigation like the back of my hand."

But he'd failed yet again. The Red Rose Killer had been on a new killing spree, and right under Oliver's nose, at that. "I don't know if this will ever end, if I can ever get past it. Maybe I should give up the FBI."

"Oliver, you can't go back to that dark place. I won't let that happen."

He smiled over at her and remembered that gentle kiss they'd shared last night. "So you'll become *my* protector now?"

"We'll protect each other," she said, the look in her eyes making him think she remembered the kiss, too. But her words dismissed that. "And we start by doing what we came here to do. We go back over this investigation, study all the reports, news briefs, questions, answers, witnesses, friends, acquaintances, everything."

He nodded and accepted that neither of them was ready for more than finding a killer right now. And that one task could bring on a lot of burnout. No need to go beyond the here and now. Work. They had work to do.

Ava put a hand on his shoulder and gave him a determined look. "I'm here and you're stuck with me until this thing is over and done."

"And after that?"

Ava stared over at him, surprise and acceptance in her dark gaze. "And after that, you're taking me for a hamburger at the Winged Java."

"That's a date," he said.

He wanted to make that date. But Oliver wasn't sure his battered heart could go beyond friendship. He'd find justice, but he wouldn't become the obsessed, half-alive man he'd been before.

He wouldn't. This time, with prayers and a new calm about him, he'd get it right. Ava's presence had grounded him.

He'd have to hold that notion tight until he knew she was safe.

Or he'd die trying.

ELEVEN

Oliver brought out a file box from his office and then, on his laptop, opened up what he'd saved on a thumb drive. "Let's get busy."

"Wow," Ava said an hour later, her coffee cup in front of her on the small desk in the den. "You were serious about being obsessed."

Not only did he have stacks of hard copies but he also had several folders saved on his hard drive and on thumb drives.

"I have every inch of anything ever written or spoken about the Red Rose Killer," Oliver admitted. "Police reports, interviews from his family and people who knew him growing up. You name it, I've studied it. So why can't I bring him in?"

"Because he's evil," Ava said, wishing she could do more. "And you did help bring him in the first time. Somehow, he escaped and now he's managing to mess with all of us."

Oliver lifted a thick file and then let it fall back down. "So evil wins?"

"No. We have to think the way he thinks."

"I'm supposed to be the expert," Oliver replied. "I've tried thinking the way he thinks. But he stays one step ahead of me. He knows the Canyon base better than I do, even though I've studied those woods and the fence that surrounds the base. He's getting in and out somehow. Thankfully, your commander has beefed up security at the gates and we have Wanted posters of Sullivan plastered outside of the gates and pretty much through the state of Texas." Shaking his head, he stared over at Ava. "How is he doing it?"

"He has help, for one," she reminded Oliver. "And we know he uses disguises and stolen IDs, but the gate patrols have been diligent checking IDs for months now. He's allegedly still in the woods now and he obviously has a good hiding place. Plus, he knows how to work the system and hide in plain sight."

"All correct," Oliver said. "But sooner or later, he has to slip up. I just wish with all my *expert* knowledge, I could make that happen."

"You *are* an expert, but you're too close to this," she said, putting her cup down on the desk. "Why don't you relax a little bit and I'll start going over this information. I know that base pretty well, too. I might see something that you haven't noticed."

"No, we're in this together."

"Oliver, you need to rest. Just rest."

She sat down beside him and urged him around. "Turn away from me."

"I'd rather turn toward you," he said with a questioning lift of his eyebrows.

"Just do as I say."

Oliver turned away with a shrug. "Yes, ma'am."

Ava put her hands on his neck and started kneading his tight muscles, acutely aware of how strong those muscles were, too.

"That does feel nice," he said, his head drooping. "If you keep that up I won't be able to concentrate on work."

"That's the whole idea," she said, finishing with a few digs that went deep. He was coiled like a rope, knotted and tightly held together. Maybe by a thread.

"Now I'm sleepy."

"See that couch over there? That's a good place to take a nap."

"But we just had breakfast."

"And we were up most of the night."

He gave her a green-eyed stare that made her think of that kiss again. "And what about you?"

"I'll be fine. Go and rest for a few minutes. It might open up some memories you've forgotten."

She watched to make sure he'd really lain down on the big couch and then turned back to the laptop and the stack of files he'd dumped on the small desk.

Then Ava started reading all about Boyd Sullivan. He'd been troubled even in childhood. From interviews from friends and neighbors, she learned his father had been a hard-nosed bully who expected Boyd to do his bidding. Boyd had killed animals for fun and picked on other kids. That was never a good thing. A scrapper, highly sensitive, disturbed, a troublemaker. His family had sent him to the military as a last resort.

He'd been forced into trying to become something he could never be, even if he thought he wanted to make it work. Ava kept reading, comparing paper reports to the ones Oliver had downloaded. After she'd read over several, it became clear to her that Boyd had issues even as a child. Then his father died when he was a teen, leaving him and his half sister, Zoe, to be raised by two different women. But Zoe had turned out okay. Why hadn't Boyd?

She wanted to understand how someone could become such a horrible person, a killer who couldn't stop. A killer who would be caught and contained, one way or another.

And, she reminded herself, a killer who now had her in his sights.

Boyd Sullivan had all the hallmarks of a sociopath and a psychopath, making him a lethal combination. Charming and convincing on the one hand and a cruel monster on the other.

Ava closed her eyes to that horror. Oliver must have suffered such grief, knowing what he knew. This monster had killed Madison out of anger and a twisted passion.

A shiver moved down her spine like a warning tickle.

The Red Rose Killer could take her life.

But there was something that scared Ava more. He could easily kill Oliver in a fit of sheer rage.

She had to find a way to stop him.

Turning to Oliver, she found him sleeping, his jaw slack against a big black pillow, his face looking younger and more relaxed as his breath lifted in soft waves. Ava got up and took an old blue throw and gently laid it over Oliver.

Then she whispered to Roscoe. The big dog lay on the floor beside the sofa, his head up. "Let him rest. He needs to find some peace."

He dreamed of Madison. She was blonde and pretty, a true Texas beauty. She wore a bright red dress and pretty sandals. Then her image changed. She was pale and gray tinged, her corpse bloody and lying on a sterile, cold autopsy table.

Dead. Madison was dead.

Oliver came awake with a groan and stared up at the woman hovering over him. Not Madison.

Ava.

"Are you all right?" she asked, concern etched across her heart-shaped face.

Ava. So different from Madison.

He couldn't fall for her. He didn't want to lose her, too. Needing to distance himself from that horrible dream and from the woman he was beginning to care way too much about, he sat up and nodded.

"I'm fine. Just a dream. What time is it?"

"Almost noon," she said. "Oliver, what kind of dream?"

"I don't want to talk about it."

Ava sat down and shrugged. "Okay, then we won't. How about some lunch?"

Running a hand over his hair, he shook his head. "No. I need to get back to work."

"Oliver, listen, I think I found something."

He got up and tugged at his wrinkled shirt. "First I need coffee." He found a fresh pot and poured a big mugful. "Okay. Talk to me."

Ava led him to the desk and then pulled up another chair. "Remember that floral Buff we found in the woods?"

"Yes. But Forensics got nothing." Oliver took a long sip of his coffee and stared at the laptop. "What did you find?"

"I hope you don't mind," Ava said, her brown eyes full of something he couldn't read—apprehension, concern? "I did some comparisons on the type of women Boyd Sullivan goes after."

"And?"

"And he seems to go for the ones who turn him down, obviously. We know that, but it becomes a quest for him and then it becomes way too personal when he thinks he's been insulted or slighted in any way."

"Yes, he's proven that with both female and male victims, so I don't see your point."

"But with the women, he seems to like the healthy, fit types."

"Okay. But the man kills at random, too, so why are you telling me this?"

Giving him a confused look after that blunt question, she said, "Back to the Buff. I pulled up photos of all the women he's hit on or been with."

Oliver's stomach recoiled, the strong coffee turning sour. He should never have told her all the intimate details about his former love life. But Ava knew everything now and there was no going back on that. "And?"

"I think I found a match to that floral Buff we found in the woods."

She pulled out a picture that Oliver recognized immediately. "This looks like the same Buff, doesn't it?" she asked.

Oliver put down his coffee mug and grabbed the picture he used to have on his dresser. "Madison," he said, his gaze moving over the image. She wore an exercise hoodie over black leggings and bright green tennis shoes. They'd been on a long run that morning and he'd snapped a picture of her downstairs right before they came up to get ready for work.

And she was wearing a floral headband that looked almost exactly like the one Ava's team had found in the woods behind the base.

Ava watched from her spot at the desk as Oliver put down his phone and stood with his hands on the back of the couch.

"Okay, I've reported in to the base and I've asked the crime techs to hold on to that headband so we can make a comparison. But I already know it's the same one."

He stayed there and looked over at Ava, the distance

between them that she'd felt since he'd woken up still cold and silent. "I don't know why I didn't see it before. Madison always wore one of those when we worked out, to keep her long hair out of her eyes."

"A lot of women do," Ava said, wishing she could erase his pain. She'd worn headbands and Buffs all of her life. "And most of the women he's targeted have had long hair and they worked out a lot."

"Including you, too, now."

He said that without an ounce of intimacy. More like FBI terms. Curt and to the point.

"Yes, but this just confirms what we already know. My point and the significance of matching this headband to the one we found is that he might have kept this one hidden away and he retrieved it when he got out of prison."

"Or someone else could have just bought the same style of headband."

"Yes, but don't you think it's mighty interesting that we found one that looks exactly like the Buff Madison is wearing in this picture?"

"I get it," Oliver said, whirling to stare out the window. Then he sat down in the chair beside her. "He loved Madison. This is all about that twisted love and his bitterness toward anyone who went up against him after she broke up with him. And the woman who is helping him could be a close match to Madison. That could be her headband. Or he might have given it to her and asked her to wear it."

"Yes, but she lost it," Ava said.

"So we go back over the list of women who've been targeted," he said, his green eyes blazing with that compulsive need to find the truth.

"Yes, just as we'd planned."

"Sullivan might also keep trophy pieces from everyone he's killed," Oliver said. "We need to look closer at the crime-scene photos as compared to the victims in other pictures before their deaths. Scarves, jewelry, medals, anything that might have gone missing. If he's regifting these trophies, we might spot something on one of these women."

Ava agreed with Oliver, but she wished that she could reach inside his heart and assure him this would all work out. But how could she guarantee that when so many people had already died at the hands of the Red Rose Killer?

She understood his putting up a wall between them. She'd wanted to do the same, and yet here they were, forced together again. Maybe God was trying to break down walls, not put more up.

After they'd studied the five victims from Dill, they didn't find much in the way of clues or missing links. Three of the five early victims had been men who'd all wronged Sullivan in some way. The two women had both dated Sullivan briefly in high school. Why had Madison Ackler taken back up with Sullivan years later when she'd claimed to be in love with Oliver?

That question might not ever have an answer, but Ava was pretty sure it was the one puzzle Oliver needed to solve.

Putting that out of her mind, Ava moved on to other scenarios. "What about fishing and camping supplies? How is he getting them? Where would he get them?"

They searched a couple of outdoor supercenters near San Antonio where Sullivan might have gone when he'd first arrived in the area.

"But how do we prove that he might have bought supplies from either of these places?" Ava asked. "He's a wanted murderer. Anyone could have recognized him."

"Maybe he didn't buy supplies," Oliver said. "Maybe he sent someone else."

"A woman."

"Exactly."

Oliver put in an order to send an agent to the two stores in question and look at security footage first. If they found any matches, they could get an order to pull up receipts to match the time of day and purchases. Then he emailed photos of Vanessa Gomez, already on Sullivan's hit list—and Yvette Crenville—who'd dated Boyd back in basic and had a public falling out with him—to headquarters and sent a report to the team at Canyon.

"It's a start," he said, giving her another rare smile.

Ava smiled back. "If we can establish Sullivan's tracks or his accomplice's movements, we can at least find a pattern and maybe figure out the way he's getting around right under our noses. Then we watch the targeted women and suspects for new jewelry or interesting accessories."

"Yes. We've searched the woods and some of the caves, but his accomplice might also be providing a getaway vehicle. He could be using a cave, too," Oliver said, getting up to stretch. "A tunnel under one of the fences."

Then he held up a hand. "The other day, right before you called about finding Turner, I spotted what I thought was a cave. I remember seeing a spark of light inside."

"But you didn't get to check it out because you rushed to help me."

"Yes, but I'm glad I did. Turner had to come first." Spinning, he said, "However, we do need to have someone check out that location and see if it leads to any other tunnels or caves."

"I can put someone on that," Ava said, reaching for her phone. "The base engineers can go over the infrastructure of the roads and boundaries and cross-check that with the geography of the land to find possible entryways."

After she finished her call, Oliver turned to stare down

at her. "Instead of running in circles, we've managed to take a step back and reevaluate this investigation and the hunt, and we've got others working to help us. We do make a good team."

Ava stood, too. "I think so." She wanted to say more, but she'd accepted that they might not last past this investigation.

So instead she brushed past him to clean up the kitchen.

But Oliver snagged her arm and tugged her back around. "How about we get out of here for a while?"

Surprised, she asked, "Are you sure?"

"Yes. I woke up in a foul mood and took it out on you. Let's go get some real dinner and, like you suggested earlier, take a break from all of this."

"I don't know."

"If you're worried about being exposed out there, don't. I know some out-of-the-way places to eat."

"It's not that. I'm not so sure we should socialize."

"We're stuck together here," he pointed out. "We can't help but socialize."

"But another dinner out? That takes things a step further, and I'm not sure either of us is ready for that."

He stood inches away. "Ava, don't give up on me. I have a lot to work through but I'm going to get there, sooner or later."

"I believe you will," she said, her prayers centered on seeing this through. "I hope so for your sake, not mine. But I hope it won't be too late for you to see that none of this is your fault."

Then she moved away and went into her room to change for dinner.

TWELVE

They waited until sundown to venture out.

Oliver guided Ava and Roscoe down side streets and through pretty back alleys full of quaint residential homes near the Riverwalk. He took her to a squatty little food trailer called The Taco Truck. It was brightly colored and tucked back in a secluded shopping area underneath towering oaks and ancient magnolias.

"How do you know your way around?" she asked, after they'd had some of the best tacos she'd ever eaten. She marveled at how Oliver made sure they blended in with other groups out on the street and along the winding paths of the Riverwalk. Marveled also at how he seemed to have ignored her concerns regarding the obvious guilt eating away at his soul. Ava knew all about that kind of guilt. It could cripple a person and ruin any chances of having a solid relationship.

"I jog a lot," he admitted, holding her hand and always keeping her near the buildings instead of the street. "After Madison died I walked a lot at night. Wound up once at this old church. I'll show it to you. It's not far from here."

A church.

Ava followed him in a zigzag through the city, taking in the blend of new and old that made San Antonio so unique. They came to a neighborhood of Spanish Eclectic homes built around the 1920s. Ava had read up on the city when she'd first come to Canyon, but she rarely made it into the downtown area. It had been over a year since she'd come to the Riverwalk for a night out with friends.

Now she was using this historical place as a cover from a killer.

But when Oliver stopped in front of a quaint Spanish-style creamy stone chapel, Ava took in a breath and stared up at the jutting steeple. For a moment, she forgot why she was standing here and allowed the beauty of the place to settle over her bones.

"Is this the church, Oliver? Is this your special place?"

He slowed to a stop under a giant oak tree. "Yes. This is where I turned back to God and vowed to turn my life around." Then he took her hand and held it tight. "This is how I'll find my way back, Ava. I don't want it to be too late. I want it to be right. Tell me you get that."

"I do," she said. "I'm trying, Oliver. I... I lost someone, too. So we've both been fighting our way out of the wilderness."

"Yes, we have. It's hard. But I need you to keep fighting, okay?"

Ava gave him a weak nod. "Okay." She glanced up at the tiny church. "It's beautiful. Why don't we go inside?"

Oliver looked into her eyes and saw that she really wanted to understand him, saw that her faith ran deep and fierce. Glad that she felt the same way he did about this little chapel, he smiled over at her.

"Sure. We could do that," he said, his heart thumping against his shirt in a fast beat. "It's never locked."

"That's a good sign."

She took his hand, guiding him now. Oliver swallowed

back the memories of that night long ago and wondered if he'd ever truly follow through with the promise he'd made in that solitary moment. He'd tried. He'd focused on work and volunteering here and there and he'd attended church when he could, but his faith still missed that essence that made him sure and solid.

When he'd heard Boyd Sullivan had escaped, Oliver had gone back down that slippery slope of doubt and bitterness.

And then he'd met Ava. The climb back up would be worth it, if he could keep her near. So he stood quietly while her gaze moved over the old chapel with the arched stained glass windows and the Mission-style facade.

The heavy, arched wood-and-metal double doors squeaked open to a muted light that carried them up the short aisle toward the altar. A stained glass backdrop of the Last Supper shimmered in reds, greens and blues, a soft yellow halo shining down on Jesus and His disciples.

The church was hushed and quiet, filled with centuries of prayers and pain, triumph and joy, and that sense of ultimate peace he'd felt the first night he'd stumbled inside. He felt an immediate peace now.

"This place hasn't changed at all."

"That's a good thing," Ava said. "It's so pretty. So peaceful. Safe. I can see why you considered it a refuge."

Oliver tugged her close as they sat down on a pew several rows back from the front. *"La Capilla de Los Perdidos."*

"The Chapel of the Lost," Ava interpreted.

They held hands and sat silent. Then Ava lowered her head and closed her eyes. Oliver did the same.

He prayed and while he prayed, he renewed his faith and asked God to help him live up to his promises and his pledges.

When he opened his eyes, Ava sat watching him with a soft smile on her lips. "I've decided that no matter what happens I will never forget you, Special Agent Davison."

"And I've decided that no matter what, I won't let you forget me, Senior Airman Esposito."

They strolled back toward the vestibule, the sound of Roscoe's paws against the wooden floor echoing out around them.

When they came out onto the sidewalk again, Ava turned to him. "I don't think I'll forget you. But things will be different when this is all over."

Oliver leaned in. "Yes, maybe then we can truly get to know each other."

And that's when the shooting started.

Drawing his handgun, Oliver pushed Ava around the corner of the church toward another street. "Run."

Another round of muted shots echoed through the night. Bullets danced off the trees and carved smoking grooves in the sidewalk all around them, a silencer making the shots whisper past without alerting anyone else.

Ava took off with Roscoe right on her heels. They turned a corner into an alleyway, the cadence of Oliver's footsteps hurrying behind them. Roscoe's low growls indicated he had picked up a familiar scent.

"Keep going," Oliver shouted, urging her on. "Up ahead."

Ava ran, tripped over an old root. Oliver righted her and they took off again, moving through the old, twisted oaks and tall cypress trees.

Oliver pushed her through a restaurant patio lined with colorful umbrellas and glanced back. "I see the shooter."

They came onto a street festival in full swing. Ava held tight to Roscoe's leash and gave the dog gentle com-

mands to keep him calm. Oliver put away his weapon
and tugged her close while they weaved in and out of
the crowd. Pulling her into a booth of jewelry and floral
hats and scarves, he peeked around the billowy dresses
hanging just inside the entryway.

The crowd merged and mingled, people laughing and
talking, but no sign of the shooter dressed in black.

"I think we lost them."

"Or they're staying out of sight." Ava took in air and
shook her hair away from her shoulders. After telling
Roscoe to stay, she turned to Oliver. "Do you think Sullivan sent someone after us?"

"Him or someone else."

"Who beside him or his accomplice would want us
dead?"

"Well, I have put a lot of people away."

"I have a feeling someone knows our every move," Ava
replied, glad for the cover of the stuffed booth.

The old woman sitting on a stool inside the opening
gave them a quiet, considering stare, her dark eyes missing nothing.

"Is there anything I can do to help?"

Ava shook her head. "Just avoiding someone unpleasant."

"Then take your time."

They huddled there inside the booth for a few more
minutes.

Oliver grabbed a colorful butterfly-embossed scarf
and paid the serene woman for it, then handed it to Ava.
"Wrap that over your hair."

Then he bought a dark baseball hat and put it over
his head.

"Thank you," the woman said after putting away the
cash. She smiled at Ava. *"Dios te bendiga."*

God bless you.

Ava nodded as she looked back. *"Gracias."*

Oliver held her close. "We'll keep close and walk back to the other side of the Riverwalk and get to my place."

Ava had ridden in the big open tour boats that served as giant taxis to the many hotels, restaurants and shops that lined the tributaries of the San Antonio River running through the city. It was a perfect night for such a ride, but too risky right now. Walking made more sense for Roscoe, too.

They circled around and crossed one of the many stone bridges over the river and then got caught in a crowd waiting for the next boat. By the time the boat was loaded with tourists and locals, they were well on their way down the path.

Oliver held her close and whispered in her ear. "Keep your head down."

Ava nodded but moved her gaze over the crowds lining the sidewalks along the waterway. Was the shooter watching them right now?

Oliver did the same, his face close to hers. Being so close only reminded her of the many reasons they needed to stay apart.

He was doing his job and just trying to protect her.

Still, one thought echoed in her head. Would he follow through on that date at the Winged Java when this was over?

"Whoever this is, they are not a trained assassin," Oliver said to Ava the next morning.

They'd made it safely back to his apartment, and Oliver had alerted the twenty-four-hour security that his female friend could possibly have a stalker. They weren't to let anyone near his apartment without calling first.

"I agree," Ava replied, staying away from the windows

now. She sat in a corner away from view, Roscoe at her feet. "We'd both be dead by now if that were the case."

He came and sat down beside her at the tiny breakfast table. "And I can tell you something else. If the Red Rose Killer wanted you dead, you wouldn't be sitting here."

"So what's his plan? To toy with me and keep everyone on alert while he does something else? Hurts someone else?"

"That's how he works," Oliver replied, picking up a piece of dry toast to take a bite. "Letting the dogs out, knowing that would be a big deal. Grabbing innocent people just so he can use their identities and uniforms to hide himself. Using this mysterious woman to run interference and cover him while he slips away."

"A woman who has to be misguided and desperate," Ava replied, wishing she could have gotten a better glimpse of the shooter in the woods and tonight. "I can't believe it's Vanessa Gomez. She seemed genuinely scared when she came by my house the other night."

"Yes, but why did she come by your house at that exact time? You were shot at right after she left."

"She didn't shoot at me and we have witnesses who can vouch for that. I think she really was concerned, or maybe she was feeling me out, since she's probably heard she's on the suspect list. And on Sullivan's list, too, for that matter."

"Maybe, but she could have been a distraction to get the shooter in place."

"Or she could be the Anonymous Blogger, digging for information."

"I don't buy that," Oliver replied. "The blogger has inside information but very little facts. More Sullivan's type of thing."

"I'm just not feeling it."

"We'll keep her on the list," Oliver said. "And we will agree to disagree."

"What about Yvette Crenville?" Ava didn't know the hyper nutritionist that well, but she'd sat through a couple of Yvette's health and wellness classes and the woman seemed ditzy to the hilt, possessive and demanding, and a bit odd. Unstable, maybe? "Yvette tends to date the wrong kind of men, from what I've heard, but she has short hair and she's kind of wiry. Not Sullivan's type."

"But she is tall and athletic," Oliver said. "She could move through the woods pretty quickly."

Ava thought about what she knew. "She has an alibi the night he first showed up and killed Landon Martelli and Tamara Peterson and then let the dogs escape."

"Yes, but a lot has happened since then. I intend to watch her more closely when we get back on the base."

Ava wanted to go back to work, but for the first time in her life she also wanted more time with a man. This man.

Too antsy from being so close to Oliver and once again almost being shot, she got up to roam around. "We also need to consider Heidi Jenks. She *is* a reporter and I've noticed the stiff competition between her and her colleague John Robinson. Maybe being the blogger is her only way of staying ahead of him. Which would mean we have a mole who is feeding her information."

"Or misinformation. And *that* person could be Sullivan's girl Friday." Shrugging, he drank some water. "What better way to keep us sniping at each other and one step behind them?"

"I just can't picture Heidi as the blogger. If she were, she'd at least verify her sources." Ava let out a sigh and shook her head. "Will we ever figure this out?"

He sat across from where she stood, his gaze holding her, reminding her of being in that church with him last night. Reminding her of things she'd put out of her mind, like a nice home and two or three children.

"I'm going to figure it out," he said, his tone quiet but firm. "I can't keep living like this, obsessed with a murderer. He killed Madison and those others in Dill. We know that. He's killed on the base. We have proof of this through DNA and other evidence. I just need to find him again and put him away for good this time."

"Would you really shoot him if you got the chance?" she asked, needing to know how far Oliver would go.

He didn't even blink. "If he tries to hurt you, yes."

Her heart tripped over itself on that one. "Oliver, you said we need to go by the book."

"I won't kill him in cold blood," Oliver said. "But I'll end this one way or another, as I've already told you. He'll either be in jail the rest of his life or he'll be six feet under."

Ava got jittery again. She couldn't trust that Oliver would be able to let this go, even if Sullivan was brought to justice again.

"We have to go back to the base tomorrow," she reminded him. "Are you still intent on doing a lineup of women?"

"If I can get Turner's parents to agree."

He stood and came around to her. "Meantime, we need to stay inside. Looks like another round of storms is coming this way."

THIRTEEN

Ava woke the next morning and came out of her room to find Oliver up and drinking coffee, his curly hair tousled and his eyes bleary.

Pulling her robe tightly against the T-shirt and leggings she'd slept in, she went to pour her own cup of brew. "Did you sleep at all?" she asked, worried about him.

"A little," he said, smiling up at her.

The reams of paper lying all around him indicated differently.

He swept a glance at her. "Did you rest?"

"Some." She'd mostly tossed and turned, but she hadn't stayed up studying videos half the night. Her thoughts had been on the man who seemed bent on protecting her and finding a killer.

He checked her over as if he didn't believe her. "You look tired."

"Not what a woman likes to hear."

He shook his head. "You have a right to be tired."

"I'll make us toast," she said, wishing she could have done a better job of tracking Boyd Sullivan, too.

She wanted to tell Oliver she *was* tired, but he looked haggard and distressed and…obsessed. He didn't need to feel guilty about how hard she'd been working, even before they'd ever joined forces. Her priorities had shifted from trying to get a promotion to stopping a vicious killer.

And fighting against her heart and the way Oliver made her feel.

Did he have the kind of staying power she needed in her life?

She didn't have much time to consider that because Oliver got up and came over to her. "Thank you."

"For what?" she said, unable to look at him.

"Breakfast. I didn't realize what time it is."

"I don't cook much, you know."

"Is that for future reference?"

"Just warning you. I'll burn this bread within minutes."

"You know, last night we were talking about what comes after this."

"And then, we were saved by bullets. Yet again."

"Don't make jokes about that, Ava."

She looked from him to the folders and documents with what she hoped was a pointed frown. "I'm sorry. I shouldn't have said that. It must have been horrible, knowing how Madison died."

He nodded and helped her butter toast. "Still is. Which is why I don't want it to happen to you."

"Did you find anything else?"

"I've established a more solid pattern. He killed her first and then, one by one, he found and shot others who he felt had wronged him. We put that together from people who knew him and remembered his volatile temper, and verified he'd had beefs with everyone he'd killed. From high school on to joining the air force and basic training, he held grudges against everyone. And he's gone after as many of them as he can."

"So he went back to Dill first and got even with people there. I guess he was still angry from being kicked out of basic and decided that since his life was spiraling out of control, it was payback time with the air force, too."

"That sums it up," Oliver said. "Now he's on a rampage and he has help. We just have to pinpoint who else is deranged enough to go along with his schemes."

"So can we predict who'll be next? I recently got added to the list. So if he's that diligent, he might go in chronological order."

"Then why are you being stalked and shot at?"

"Because the shooter might not be Sullivan or his woman friend. Maybe it's someone else entirely. Maybe we have a copycat on our hands."

Oliver took the toast she put on a plate with some fruit she'd sliced yesterday. "Someone else who hangs out in the woods and leaves a rose and a note?"

"We have to consider that possibility since people tend to take advantage of this type of thing. But that doesn't add up, does it?"

"I don't know. You might be onto something." He took a big bite of toast. "But first, breakfast, because this is the best toast I've ever eaten."

She burst out laughing at that.

"Let's get back on to our investigation," she said. "We'll keep digging, keep tracking, keep praying."

"I like the way you think."

Ava ate her toast, wishing she could say what she was really thinking. Oliver wasn't going to give up on this investigation, and she understood his reasons. But where did that leave them?

They were on the road back to the base by noon, but Oliver wished he could prolong the weekend. The light Sunday traffic made the drive go by faster, so he couldn't stall much longer, but he sure liked being with her. At least they'd had a little downtime, if he didn't count the shooter by the Riverwalk.

"I missed church," Ava said, her gaze sweeping over Oliver. "Have you ever met Pastor Harmon? He's married with two sets of twins, one of them a girl. And all of them under the age of ten."

"I don't think I have," Oliver replied. "I… I don't go to church on base. But I'm impressed about the twins. He must have a lot of patience."

"He and his wife both. They're a great couple. Good to talk to about anything."

"Glad to hear that." He watched the road, always checking. "Do you think I need spiritual counseling?"

"Can't we all use that at times? You've been through a lot, Oliver."

"Yes. And you know all about me now. Why don't I know more about you?"

"You're turning the tables," she said. "Okay, I'll lay off for now."

His expression softened but his words were firm. "I still want to hear your story."

"One day," she promised, looking uncomfortable. Why was it so hard for her to talk about herself? No doubt changing the subject, she asked him, "Do you attend at the Chapel of the Lost?"

"When I'm not deep into a case."

They made it onto the interstate that would take them west of town. Oliver glanced back to do a check and saw a black sedan approaching at a rapid pace.

"Ava, slide down in the seat."

"Why?" she asked, turning.

"Don't look back," he said, watching the vehicle behind them. "I think our shooter has found us again."

Ava did as he asked and scooted down. "Are you serious?"

"Someone is riding my bumper and I don't think it's a little old lady coming home from church."

The vehicle sped up but Oliver couldn't make out the person inside since the driver was wearing a dark baseball hat and sunglasses. "Looks like the same car that followed us on base the other night."

"Should we call for help?" Ava asked, taking a glance in the passenger-side mirror.

"Not yet," Oliver said. He weaved his car in and out of the sparse traffic. "Let me make sure I'm not just imagining things."

The black sedan followed, quickly and expertly.

In the rear, Roscoe woofed, sensing an adventure.

"If that's our shooter, he or she seems to know how to tail people."

"Practice makes perfect," Ava said, her tone full of that fierce bravery he knew so well.

"Yeah, I'm thinking that, too."

"What are we going to do? Let them chase us all the way to the base?"

"We could."

"I can alert the gate," she said, going into action.

"Ava, wait on that," he said. "I think I'll try to lose them."

"But then we won't know who they are."

"That doesn't matter right now. I have to put your safety first."

"Forget that," she said. "We have to do something."

She unfastened her seat belt. "I'm going to the back."

"No, you are not," Oliver said, grabbing her arm. "Ava, buckle up and stay down. I'm going to find a way to get us out of this."

She glared at him but refastened her seat belt. Then she told Roscoe to lie down.

Oliver breathed a sigh of relief. "Good. I can't drive and watch out for you at the same time."

Looking contrite, she glanced in the side mirror. Then she sat up. "Oliver, I think I saw someone on the passenger side."

"Okay, stay down. When the shooting starts, I need you to dive down as low as you can."

"Okay. But what about you?"

"I'll be fine."

He didn't plan on letting them get that close.

He kept zigzagging, but the car stayed with them, the driver not moving a muscle but keeping the car close. What did the driver hope to accomplish? And how had they found Ava and him?

As if she'd read his mind she said, "They must have waited outside your apartment-complex gate."

"This is growing tedious," Oliver said. "But we're going to keep moving and hope they'll either back off or play chicken with us."

"I don't mind playing chicken as long as we win," Ava retorted.

She'd do that. Ram them and stare them down.

That worried Oliver to the point that he figured he'd need to play it safe to keep her out of the fray.

But the vehicle advanced and just tapped the back bumper.

"Now they're getting serious," Oliver said.

He made it off the main road, taking an exit that would bring them around to the base. "Hold on, Ava. I'm about to break the law."

Ava nodded and grabbed the door handle. "I'm good."

Oliver peeled out and took off to the right of the two-lane road, then passed a farmer in a pickup truck. Speeding away, he checked the rearview mirror and saw the dark car behind the farmer.

"Here they come," Ava warned, her gaze on the side mirror and her body language showing she was ready to brace for impact.

Oliver nodded. "I'll be ready for them."

He sped up and hit twenty miles over the speed limit, all the while watching for cars up ahead.

They rounded a curve and for a moment, the sedan disappeared. But Oliver looked up as they were cresting a hill. "Moving closer. He'll come after us on the long stretch."

Ava glanced in the mirror to her right. "Let's rodeo."

Oliver shook his head. Did the woman have no fear?

The car approached close enough that Oliver spotted the shooter aiming out the passenger-side window. "Stay down, Ava," he said again. "I'm going to do a spin."

"I need your gun," she said, her tone full of grit.

"No."

"Yes."

Oliver took his handgun out of the shoulder holster, but he didn't give it to her. "I can shoot and drive at the same time."

"Oliver!"

"Stay down."

Placing the gun in his lap, he hit the button to the window on his side to open it.

Oliver waited until the right moment to slow a bit. When the car approached and tapped him this time, he was ready. He hit the brakes for a split second, causing the other car to slam hard against his vehicle. Then he went into a turn that brought him into the other lane and almost ran them into the ditch. But he held the wheel and then reached for his weapon.

After that, he started shooting through the window, his other hand guiding the vehicle.

Ava held tight, her eyes wide, bullets whirling all around them.

Oliver completed the one-eighty and shot another round, which caused the driver to veer away. He and Ava watched while the other vehicle came up on a slow-moving van.

Then they heard the screeching of tires and saw the black sedan slide into the low ditch to avoid hitting the van. The car moved through a field, dust and rocks spewing up behind it.

"We've got 'em now," Ava said, triumph in her words.

But the two people in the car got out and took off running into the sparse woods behind an old barn.

"And there they go," Oliver said, hitting the steering wheel in rapid palm slaps. "I can't tell who it is since they look like ninjas. Exactly how Turner Johnson remembered them."

"Should we go after them?"

"No. Too risky out here," Oliver said. "But they left the car. We can at least take a picture of the license plate and send it in. Then we'll call the locals and report their bad driving habits."

"I hope they run across a rattlesnake," Ava said, her gaze on the now still, smoking car. "Do you think that was Boyd Sullivan and his handy helper?"

"Probably," Oliver said. "The shooting was bad."

He called in their location. "Now we wait."

"No, now I call Westley and get some help out here," Ava replied. "Meantime, I have Roscoe."

"The car is stolen," Master Sergeant Westley James told Ava an hour later. "We'll notify the owner. Maybe they can shed some light on how it went missing."

Ava held Roscoe's leash. They'd tracked a scent into the hills across from the field but lost it at the crest of the first bluff. "Nothing on the car?"

"No prints to speak of," Westley replied. "They must have both been wearing gloves."

"They were covered from head to toe," Oliver said, his frown edged with frustration. "I got off a round but I don't know if I hit one of them."

Westley looked from him to Ava. "So tell me about the shooting in San Antonio."

Ava's gaze slammed into Oliver's. "You told him about that?"

"I had to, Ava. You're still in danger."

She went through the scenario. "We got away and no civilians were hurt, thankfully."

"So much for staying safe," Westley said. "But we might be able to find something to connect that car to Boyd Sullivan."

"It had to be him driving that car," Ava said, her stomach still queasy from all the excitement. "I just want to know who his wingman is."

"Or his wing woman," Oliver added. "We need that lineup, and soon."

Ava watched him stalk away. "He's running on thin air, sir."

"I can see that," Westley said. "We'd hoped this time away with you would calm him down."

"We survived, but now we know Sullivan or someone who might be helping him is somehow tapping our every move."

Westley nodded. "Let me go talk to the locals about towing the car. It's evidence for now."

Ava saluted him and then rubbed Roscoe's head. "We make a good team, don't we?"

Roscoe woofed his agreement and stared up at her with doleful eyes.

"*We* make a good team, too," Oliver said from behind her, his expression full of a longing that tore through her.

Ava held his gaze, her whole being aware of how this man had changed her.

"But we haven't been very successful so far," she said. "And I'm not sure you can ever move on until you can find some peace and let go."

"You mean, let go of the Red Rose Killer?" he asked, following her to the row of official vehicles lined up on the highway.

"No," she said, turning her head to look him in the eyes. "I mean Madison Ackler. Are you sure you didn't really love her, Oliver?"

FOURTEEN

Ava was back at work but bored. She'd been confined to desk duty for this week. Her superiors didn't think it was a good idea to have her roaming around the woods while a shooter seemed intent on going after her. She didn't dare tell anyone until she could verify it, but each time she went out anywhere on base, she got the feeling someone was watching her. Waiting for her.

While she was away, no one came snooping at her house so the decoy didn't work. But going back there could be dangerous.

Was the killer waiting for the right opportunity to take her out?

Not today. Here she sat, doing paperwork, studying training updates and annoying the other K-9 handlers by offering to do their work for them. She and Roscoe had worked through several practice sessions, too.

She was also staying away from Oliver.

Each day, they were briefed on the status of the Red Rose Killer and other investigations. Since Ava hadn't been called out on any rescues, she stayed in the secure areas of the training center. But no one had seen any sign of Boyd Sullivan since last week, and she and Oliver had no proof that the two people who'd chased them were Sullivan and his accomplice. The owner of the stolen car had been out of town and had come home to find his house ransacked and his car missing. No prints and no security footage. Another rabbit hole.

They'd sent people to check several outdoor superstores in the areas surrounding San Antonio, so maybe they'd get a hit from one of them and be able to go through the store security tapes and find a receipt or two. As long as the store was willing to cooperate, they wouldn't need a warrant.

Oliver went out every day, searching for any signs of Boyd Sullivan. The woods had grown quiet since they'd found Turner Johnson. Ava figured Sullivan had watched them and had either followed them into the city or had someone follow them.

Unable to get through security at Oliver's apartment building, that person, or persons, had waited until Ava and Oliver had made a move.

Now Oliver was beating himself up for taking her out of the apartment and exposing her to a shooter. Why did he seem to want to carry every kind of guilt on his shoulders?

He'd never really answered her when she'd asked if he'd loved Madison. Earlier he'd claimed he didn't, but what if he truly did? Could that be the thing that held him back? That kept him invested in finding the killer?

Now, three days later, Ava sat at her desk and thought about everything that had happened over the last couple of months. Oliver's silence seemed to prove her point. She'd stared at the map on the wall that contained all the photos of the victims and those who'd been threatened. Connected with thumb tacks and strings of colored twine, they told the tale of the Red Rose Killer's murderous rampage.

Oliver was right. This shouldn't be so hard, but Sullivan knew how to slip in and out and stay under the radar, a true trait of a serial killer. But Oliver believed in the one thing that brought down most psychopaths. Sooner or later, their egos made them slip up.

Oliver didn't want to move on, because he wanted to find the killer. But he also had a load of guilt because of Madison's death, either because he hadn't really loved her, or because he did love her and he was still grieving.

But he's the one who opened up to you.

Maybe it was time for her to take the next step. Oliver had tried so many times to get her to talk to him.

She'd call him tonight and invite him over to dinner. Except that her house was still being monitored in case her shooter returned. Oliver had made sure of that, even if he'd pulled himself off of guarding her.

It was time to confront the man.

They could meet at the Winged Java. A lot of friends met there. And that would work better. It was a less intimate setting for opening up her heart.

Her cell rang, causing Ava to sit up straight in her desk chair. "Esposito."

"We need to meet and talk."

Oliver. Did he have a built-in radar on her?

"Hello to you, too."

"Hi," he said on a long breath. "I need to see you."

"Uh, okay. The Winged Java?"

"No. I'll come there. Meet me in the parking lot."

"Okay."

"Why the subterfuge?" she asked once she and Roscoe were outside of the K-9 training center.

Oliver gave her the once-over, his eyes telling her nothing. "Have you forgotten what we've been through?"

"No, but this is different."

"I wanted privacy, but I also wanted a wide-open area so I'll know no one is listening."

"Okay." She glanced around, that creepy feeling overcoming her again, and followed him to a bench near the main building. "What's going on, Oliver?"

He placed his hands on his lap. "I tried to love her. I wanted to love her. But my job was the thing. I loved my job more than I loved Madison. She wanted more and I tried to give her that. But I didn't have strong feelings for her."

Ava absorbed that while she watched the road and the grounds. "So if you don't love her, do you resent her for lying to you?"

"Yes," he said. "Her death was horrible. I want you to know that this is my burden to bear and that not having that last conversation with her and hearing the truth has bothered me a lot. I've turned back to my faith and I'm working my way through the grief and the resentment. I try to be honest with people, but…I wasn't honest with Madison and she sure wasn't honest with me. She turned to someone else for comfort and we both made a mess of things."

Ava saw the pain and grief in his eyes. He was the type of man who needed answers, but he'd never have answers from Madison.

So he searched for the truth in his work. He wanted to find Boyd Sullivan again to try to get those answers. Last time, the hunt had been fast and furious and had ended with Oliver being in on the arrest of the man who'd murdered the woman he'd tried to love. This time, he'd want more. He'd want to get to the bottom of things so he could finally let this go.

"Do you think saving me will be atonement for the

fact that you couldn't save her? Or that you couldn't have that last conversation with her?"

"That's part of it, of course."

"What's the other part, Oliver?" she asked, her heart bursting for that truth he held so high.

"I want to protect you," he said. "It's that simple."

"You are anything but simple," she replied. "I don't know how to handle you."

"Why don't you start by being honest with me, Ava."

"About what?"

"About what really happened when that chopper went down."

Well, she had wanted to see him and tell him about the tragic helicopter crash that had changed her life. He was here and he was ready to listen. But was she ready to talk?

Ava stared down at her boots. "I don't think—" She stopped, listening. Did she hear footsteps crunching in the mulch by the crape myrtles? Or was it only squirrels frolicking?

"Do you want to go somewhere more private?" he asked.

She glanced around and understood why he needed the open air. It was hard to breathe through this. Her emotions were on edge. "No. It's better here. I can't fall apart here."

"Ava—"

"No, you need to know, Oliver. It's nothing mysterious, nothing against my record or anything like that."

"I didn't think it would be," he said. "Just talk to me, Ava."

"Nothing much to tell." She took a deep breath and began her story. "The chopper had a four-person crew and some Search-and-Rescue personnel looking for three missing soldiers in a remote part of Afghanistan. Should have been an in-and-out extraction since we had their location and had communicated with them over a secure two-way evader locator and were ready to roll. We verified their location and dropped down, and they were climbing aboard when someone launched an attack."

Oliver listened, a slight nod his only encouragement, but his hand hovered near hers on the bench.

"We got blasted and things turned nasty pretty quickly." She stopped, took in a breath, kept an eye on Roscoe. The dog's ears had gone up and he had his nose in the air. "Julian and I had become friends from the start. We were in basic training together and both wanted to be pilots. We were crew members—he was the gunner and I worked as a flight engineer. We spent our spare time together. We were both the same rank but when we…got closer, we decided to be extra careful, just in case." She shrugged. "He was as ambitious as me. So it was kind of a competition."

Oliver gave her a gentle smile. "But you were in love?"

"We fell in love, yes. But we were in the middle of a war zone." Remembering Julian's olive skin and gentle brown eyes, she shook her head. "I'll never know what might have happened once we got back stateside." Pulling away, she said, "We got hit with several rounds and then the chopper started spiraling out of control. The pilot was shot and when I looked around, Julian's eyes met mine. He gave me the sweetest smile and then…he just toppled over onto the gun."

Oliver's expression mirrored the pain that would always be inside her heart. "I'm sorry."

"Yes, me too," she said, the bitterness tasting like bile. "I don't remember much after that. I woke up in triage and then I was in and out of consciousness until we got to Germany. I had contusions and a broken leg and everything was kind of fuzzy for a while. But when they told me Julian was dead, a lot of it came rushing back."

She wiped her eyes. "I wish it hadn't. I wish I didn't remember him every day of my life."

She saw a flicker of something unattainable in Oliver's eyes. "So you need answers, too?"

"No, I need memories. Good memories. Ours were all wrapped up in death and fire and go, go, go."

"An adrenaline rush."

She nodded again, tears burning her eyes. "I'll never know about those soft, sweet memories."

"I'm sorry you had to go through that," he said. "But you pulled through and you're great at what you do now."

"I pulled through only after a lot of therapy and someone introducing me to the Working Dog program. I had to work hard to qualify and that saved me. But it didn't prepare me for someone like you walking into my life." She lifted her chin. "I've been coasting along on a routine that kept me stable and steady and now…I'm shaky and not so sure about my future."

"You have a future, if I can keep you alive."

"You see, that's it, right there. Your need to watch out for me. I'm not Madison, Oliver. I can take care of myself. What I can't risk is losing someone else I care about."

He leaned back, his eyes going dark. "So that's why you're avoiding me? We've been forced together and we're dealing with the horror of a serial killer on the prowl."

"Isn't that enough to do anyone in?"

He gave her a look that told her he understood her now, his eyes full of a misty realization. "More than enough. But, Ava, we're both stronger now. We've lost a lot, been through things no one wants to go through, but we've also gained a lot. Wisdom, caution, understanding, empathy. And I think we've both grown stronger in our faith."

"But can we truly heal, Oliver?" she asked, her heart doing that fast beat that told her she was close to panic.

"We signed up for this kind of life—the kind that takes over your soul at times. I flew a lot of missions over there and they didn't all turn out good. We saved a lot of soldiers but we lost some, too."

"And I've put away a lot of bad people but some of them got away," he replied. "We can't let that define us. We have to keep fighting."

"I want to keep fighting," she admitted. "But what if that ambition, that need to make things right, destroys us in the process?"

"Are you worried about me? About how I won't let go of this chase?"

"Yes, I am," she said. "I know you want to capture Boyd Sullivan and I sure want that, too. But there comes a time when you just have to give over the power and let someone else take the lead."

"But we're going to find him. And soon. That doesn't mean you and I can't be close. Friends, at least, for now."

"And what about later? Will you disappear when we come down off that rush?"

"You don't seem to understand," he said, his eyes burning with a distant fire. "You give me the same kind of rush, but in a much better way."

"I can't do that if you wear yourself down looking for a man who might not ever come out of the shadows. What then, Oliver? Will you keep on chasing him until you're the one who gets killed? Do you want that more than you want us?"

He gave her a shocked stare. "Ava, are you asking me to remove myself from the search to find the Red Rose Killer?"

FIFTEEN

Oliver waited for her to respond.

But Ava seemed distracted. She kept an eye on Roscoe.

"I can't stop midstream," he said, wishing there was some other way. "You know how this works."

She nodded and turned back to him, her eyes misty and filled with dread and concern. "Yes, I do know how it works. That's why there can't be an *us* until you're done with him."

Trying to understand, Oliver sat up straight. She wasn't in the mood for this discussion and maybe he wasn't either. "I will be done with him if I can ever find the man."

"You'll keep chasing him all over Texas. He's a survivalist, Oliver. He can stay on the lam for months, possibly years."

"I'll find him, and soon," Oliver said, determination making his tone sharp.

Ava stood up. "Okay, we'll go with that. I want him put away again, too. He's wreaked havoc on this base and the state of Texas for way too long now. But I've been shot at and harassed and I have guards outside my apartment day and night and you taking me on as your responsibility. So I'm forced to stay near the training center. Which is good, I guess, since I'm pouring over documents and electronic files. Maybe I'll find a clue that can lead us to him. Maybe not. But I'm going to do my job, too."

"Is this a brush-off, Ava?" he asked. "Are you saying you'll find him and save me the task?"

"What I'm saying is that I have a stake in this, too. I can pour myself into my work, same as you."

When she turned to leave, Oliver caught up with her. "That sounds a lot like a challenge, Ava."

"It could be. But I'm tired of sitting at my desk. If I have to drag Boyd Sullivan in by his hair, I'll do it. I can't function this way anymore."

Oliver's heart skipped a few beats. She was too reckless for her own good. "Don't say that. Don't even think it."

"I'll be careful," she said. "Meantime, you get on that lineup you're so determined to provide."

He stopped her. "I can't. The Johnsons refuse to let Turner do it. They won't put him through anything else that could add to his trauma. They say he's been through enough and he still has nightmares."

Some of the fire went out of her. "Don't we all?"

Oliver wanted to take her in his arms. "Ava…"

"Don't say it." She turned to go back inside. "Just let me work on this, Oliver. Let me figure it all out."

"Alone?" He couldn't let her go.

"Yes. Alone. Same way I've always done things."

"That's too dangerous."

"Oliver, I'll be okay. You do your job and I'll do mine, all right?"

He reached for her, his hand on her shoulder while he leaned in. "I'm sorry about Julian. He sounds like a good man."

Ava resisted pulling away. "He was a good man. He

died too young. But he died doing what he loved, fighting bad guys. We lost several good people that day."

"You need to take care of yourself."

"And so do you," she said. Then she headed back to the building. But just before she reached the door, Roscoe alerted and barked a warning. Ava whirled, meeting Oliver's gaze.

"Inside," he said, drawing his gun. "Get inside."

Oliver heard someone running away.

Ava heard it, too, and ignored his warning to go inside the building. "Find," she said to Roscoe. The big dog leapt into the shrubbery near the building, his barks loud and clear. Someone had been in the bushes, listening to them.

Ava and Oliver both rushed around the corner just as a car motor revved to life. Roscoe stood at the sidewalk, barking at the vehicle that turned the corner before Oliver got a good look at the plates.

Shaking her head, Ava called Roscoe back. "I guess now even this place isn't safe for me anymore."

Ava hadn't slept well that night but at least she was back at her place, Roscoe by her side. She'd dreamed of the chopper crash and Julian's smile. But in the dream, Julian turned into Oliver and they were running through the woods with someone right on their heels. Then she saw a little boy moving through the shadows, but when she called out to him, her voice was barely above a whisper.

She'd woken in a cold sweat, fear clawing at her. Not fear for herself, but a new fear. Turner Johnson had seen the bad man and he'd heard the woman talking. He'd heard them fighting and arguing.

What if Sullivan decided to track him down after all?

Who had been listening to her and Oliver there near the training center today? They'd searched the area and found nothing. The dark compact car had disappeared into traffic.

And they'd both been too distracted even to know they were being watched. But she'd felt it. She should have been more alert.

She gave up on sleep and tried to focus on work, but she finally fell asleep on the couch. When she woke, groggy and more confused than ever, she went out to get the paper. Roscoe went along with her for a quick walk around the yard so he could have his own break. She had the paper and was halfway back up the short drive when she saw Yvette Crenville jogging by.

The other woman looked even more gaunt than last time Ava had seen her, almost malnourished in spite of her job as a nutritionist. Remembering from her research that Yvette had briefly dated Boyd Sullivan, Ava had to wonder again if Yvette could be his helper. But they'd had a horrible and very public fight right before he left basic. Besides, she and Oliver had watched Yvette's routine and found nothing out of the ordinary. But that didn't mean she wasn't sneaking out at all hours. She might be covering her tracks too well for them to see anything.

Had Sullivan rekindled things with Yvette after his escape the same way he'd rekindled things with Madison once he found her again? Would he eventually kill this woman when he was done with her?

Ava kept smiling as Yvette approached, all the while trying to figure out if Yvette had been the one shooting at her.

She certainly had the tall, slender frame of someone who could probably be a fast runner. But the shooter in the woods had been dressed in bulky sweats and a hoodie. Ava had never seen the shooter's eyes or hair. Yvette had short, choppy blond hair that stood out all around her face. Not Boyd's usual type at all. But he could have changed types to suit his purposes.

Deciding to test that theory, she waited for Yvette to pass, and then waved, "Hey, I haven't seen you around for a while."

Yvette slowed and ran in place, but stayed on the sidewalk. "Hey, Ava. You missed my last class on the low-carb diet, not that you need to worry about that."

Ava held Roscoe's leash and laughed. "Yes, I've been kind of busy."

"So I heard." Yvette stopped jogging in place and took a deep breath. "Me, too. Keeping a low profile right now." Pushing at the spikes of hair around her forehead, Yvette added, "I've had a lot of things going on. I just broke up with my boyfriend."

Ava felt Roscoe bristle, but the big dog didn't show any outward signs of distress. He'd never been around Yvette, so maybe he was reacting to her as a stranger. But then, animals picked up on hostility, too, and she'd heard Yvette complain more than once about all the "mutts" on the loose. Obviously, the woman didn't like dogs a whole lot.

"I'm sorry to hear that," Ava replied, remaining neutral. "I didn't know you were in a serious relationship."

Yvette's grunt and frown showed a hint of anger. "Apparently, neither did he."

Ava noted the grimace and the hostility of Yvette's statement. "I'm sorry, Yvette. Relationships are always complicated."

Yvette's gaze scanned the quiet street. "Yeah, I guess so. At least now I have more free time on my hands. Anyway, I heard about the incident in the woods. You rescued that little boy."

"Yes, I did," Ava said, wary of the concern in Yvette's

words. "But I had a lot of help. The whole team was in on the search."

"And the search for the Red Rose Killer, too," Yvette said with a delicate shudder. "It's hard to sleep at night, knowing he might still be out there. Why hasn't that hunky FBI agent hurried up and done his job?"

"We won't give up on finding him," Ava replied, wondering if Yvette was deliberately baiting her about Oliver.

"I also heard you and what's-his-name, Owen, Olson, have grown close."

"Special Agent Oliver Davison," Ava replied. "And we're friends. Chasing someone through the woods does that to people."

"Oh, I see." Yvette winked and checked the street both ways. "Hopefully, the killer is long gone and you'll never have to go back into the woods again. It can be dangerous out there. I worry about that kid, too."

Again, Roscoe bristled. Ava felt a chill moving down her spine. Just her imagination and lack of sleep? Or did Roscoe recognize Yvette's scent?

At what sounded like a threat to both her and Turner Johnson, she stiffened her spine and stared Yvette down. "If Sullivan returns here, I'll be ready to go anywhere to bring him in."

"You're so brave," Yvette retorted with a smile. "And I need to be gone myself. Busy day, as always." Running backward, she shouted, "Let's do lunch someday soon." Then she frowned and pointed to a neighbor's trash can. "Messy around here."

Always the complainer, from what Ava had heard about Yvette. That, coupled with the cryptic conversation and the way Roscoe had silently alerted, made Ava wonder yet again about Yvette. Could she be sneaking out to help Boyd Sullivan?

Ava made a note to check into Yvette's schedule again, but for now she could report back to Oliver that she'd encountered one of their suspects.

And that she'd gotten the creeps from that encounter.

Then she remembered she'd pulled away from Oliver. How easy it had become for her to think about telling him things first.

But she was on her own now and she would report to her superiors, especially her concerns involving the boy. She had to stay away from Oliver until they were both done with the Red Rose Killer. Only then could she be sure about him, and only then could she decide if she was ready for another relationship.

Once she was back inside the house, Ava poured herself a cup of coffee, then opened her laptop to her email. And found another update from the Anonymous Blogger.

Seems the FBI Agent and the female Search-and-Rescue crew member are still at odds, even after they emerged as heroes after a dangerous rescue of a little boy a few days ago in the Canyon Base Reserve wooded area. Why are they still arguing about the Red Rose Killer? Why aren't they out there finding the man? These two appear to be more competitive than capable. And who keeps trying to shoot them? Who is on their suspect list now?

Ava let out a groan. Had the blogger been listening in on their conversation yesterday?

But this was not good. Ava was already being scrutinized and watched for her protection. This kind of attention would only bring her more into the limelight and fuel the killer's keen need to make her life go from bad to worse.

Boyd Sullivan had been jealous of Oliver Davison once

before, and that had not ended well. She had to stay away from Oliver, not only for herself but for his safety, too.

Oliver had been staying in the base hotel this week so he could get out early each morning with a fresh team to scour the woods and surrounding areas. So far, he'd found no signs of the Red Rose Killer, not even a campfire or bit of trash left in a cave. Oliver had even gone back to the big cave where he'd seen a light the day Ava had found Turner Johnson. Nothing in there but bats and spiders, but it could have served as a good place to hide.

"We could go in deeper," one of his men had suggested. "Some of these caverns go far into the earth."

Working on that angle, Oliver now sat studying topography and geological maps of the Hill Country around the base and San Antonio. What if Sullivan was somehow moving through one of those caverns that lead right underneath the base's back fence?

Before he could wrap his brain around that, his cell rang.

"Davison."

"Agent Davison, this is Lieutenant Nick Donovan. The blogger has posted something new."

"What, Lieutenant?"

Nick read him the short blog post. "Have you and Ava been at odds again?"

That was an understatement. "We've been discussing this investigation a lot, as you well know," Oliver replied. "I need to call her before she hears about this."

"I reckon you do," Nick replied. "Talk to you later."

Oliver ended the call and reached for his phone.

This would set off Boyd Sullivan.

He had to stay away from Ava for her own good.

But that didn't stop him from hitting her contact number on his phone.

Ava didn't pick up. Instead, her phone rang and rang and then went to voice mail.

Rather than leave a message, Oliver finished getting dressed and headed out to find her.

SIXTEEN

"I have a special assignment for you, Esposito," Master Sergeant Westley James said to Ava when she reported for duty after seeing the blogger's latest post.

Wondering if she was going to be reprimanded, Ava nodded. "Yes, sir." He'd probably read the Anonymous Blogger's latest report and decided Ava wasn't qualified to continue the search. But she had decided that she and Oliver weren't going to be seeing much of each other outside of work from now on. Things were getting too mixed-up. So she would make that clear to her superior.

"I need you to head out to the airfield and stand by at the main hangar," Westley explained. You'll be escorting Senior Airman Isaac Goddard to wait for a plane that should be bringing in the dog he's been trying to locate." He checked his watch. "Scheduled to arrive at 1100 hours."

"You mean they found Beacon?" she asked, excited for her friend Isaac. Beacon had saved Isaac's life and he'd been searching for the dog ever since he'd returned stateside.

"We think," Westley said. "Just stay with Isaac, will you? He's been having a hard time lately."

"Sure, sir," Ava replied. This wasn't the assignment

she'd expected, but she was more than willing to help her friend who suffered from PTSD. "I'll leave Roscoe in his kennel in the car so the other dog won't get agitated."

"Good idea." Then Westley opened the office door and turned back to Ava. "Oh, and Special Agent Davison is going with you."

"May I ask why, sir?" Ava asked, shocked. So much for avoiding Oliver.

"He called looking for you," Westley replied, his tone as neutral as the paint color on the wall. "I told him you'd been over at the kennels helping tag and exercise some of the dogs we've picked up but you were about to head over to the flight line. He said he's on his way."

"I don't need Special Agent Davison to go with me, sir."

"I'm going with you whether you like it or not."

She whirled to find Oliver standing at the door to Westley's office. "That's not necessary."

"We need to talk, and we can do that on the way," Oliver replied, walking into the room. "I've been considering your concerns regarding the Johnson boy."

Ava looked back at Westley and almost protested. But he gave her a stern stare that reminded her he was her superior. "Orders, Esposito."

"Yes, sir."

Westley made to leave but stopped outside his door to speak to Captain Blackwood's sixteen-year-old daughter, Portia, who happened to be walking by. "On your way to hang with your dad?" he asked.

The girl's disdain was palatable and the expression on her face showed boredom and aggravation. Ava had heard she was a handful. But she felt some sympathy for the girl since Portia's mother had died last year and her life had changed completely when she'd come to live with Justin, the father she didn't really know.

Portia twirled and smacked her chewing gum. "Forced to hang around like I'm a kid."

Westley's smile was patient. "Your dad will enjoy that, at least."

Portia tossed her long blond hair. "I seriously doubt that." Then she glanced into the office where Ava and Oliver stood. Giving them an eye roll, she took off, her black lace-up boots clacking on the floor.

"Teenagers," Westley said with a shake of his head. "I'll want a full report on what you find at the hangar, Esposito."

"Yes, sir."

When the sergeant had left, Ava whirled to Oliver. "Why are you here?"

He pushed back his hair and gave her his own eye roll. "Because I've been looking for you all morning and I'd like to discuss some things with you."

"I've been right here, under house arrest."

"Protective custody," he corrected.

"Call it what you want. I've scrubbed kennels, gone through the obstacle courses with the dogs, caught up Roscoe on training hours, his shots and a good bath, and I've filed away more paperwork than I ever care to see again."

"So you need a diversion," Oliver said, walking with her to the parking lot, Roscoe following obediently.

"Yes, maybe. But you don't have to be a part of that diversion."

"I was concerned about you. I haven't seen you since that scare yesterday, and you haven't returned my calls."

Ava handed Roscoe up into his kennel and made sure he was secure before heading to the driver's side. "I'm okay, Oliver. Which you know, since I've seen you checking with my security detail."

"Until that brief conversation yesterday, you've been avoiding me."

"I thought that was the other way around. You've been busy searching for the Red Rose Killer and you've been avoiding me. Besides, each time we're together we make things more dangerous for everyone. Someone was here yesterday and they got away yet again."

"Another reason I wanted to talk to you yesterday, but we got interrupted."

"What about?"

"I wasn't avoiding you, Ava. I was trying to stay away from you. And I'm pretty sure you were trying to do the same for me."

She shot him a questioning look as they hopped into her SUV. "Why, besides the obvious?"

"Because the Red Rose Killer has a grudge against me and I thought if I stayed away from you—"

"He'd come after you instead and end the grudge?"

"Something like that, but he seems to have disappeared off the face of the earth."

Ava headed north on Canyon Drive. "And I was avoiding you and staying out of sight so he wouldn't come after you while he's trying to eliminate me."

"We've got to stop avoiding each other that way," Oliver said, his eyes dark with emotion and worry. "I was stupid, okay. I thought if I threw myself back into work, I could forget you. To protect you."

"That is kind of stupid."

"What's your excuse?"

"I was trying to protect you and to let you do your thing. Because you need to get him out of your system before I can be in your life."

"You drive a hard bargain."

"Yeah, well, I guess I do. I don't like losing people."

"You won't lose me."

"You can't make that kind of promise, Oliver. Look, let's just pick up Isaac and get to the hangar."

"Okay," Oliver replied while, out of habit, they both checked for any tails behind them. "At least Isaac will get some good news. He's going to see Beacon again today."

"That's not Beacon."

Isaac Goddard's green eyes held disappointment and frustration while he stared down at the dog Ava held on a leash near the kennel he'd traveled in. "Is this some kind of joke? Is someone trying to pull one over on me and make me think this is Beacon?"

Ava glanced at Oliver and then back to Isaac. "We had confirmation that this might be your dog, but no one could say for sure until he arrived and you had a chance to look him over."

Isaac looked contrite and lowered his head, his wavy sandy-brown hair glimmering in the sunlight. "He's a German shepherd all right." He petted the curious dog's furry head and checked him up close. "But he's not Beacon."

The dog sniffed at Isaac and let out a soft cry. Isaac smiled at that, but stood and pulled away.

Oliver bent down to pet the scrawny dog's dark brown fur. The dog woofed and licked Oliver's hand. "Sorry, man," he said to Isaac. "I guess you'll have to keep trying."

Isaac shook his head and backed away. "I'm never gonna find him. It's important that I do, though." Shrugging, he said, "I know it's silly but…Beacon belongs with me."

"Then don't give up," Ava said, her hand on her friend's

arm. "Isaac, remember how far you've come. You survived and Beacon saved your life. It might take a long time to find him, but you can search as long as you need to."

"Yeah, I reckon so," Isaac said. "Let's get this guy to the training center. Maybe he can be somebody's dog."

"But not yours?" Ava asked, hoping Isaac would change his mind. The dog kept looking up at him, as if eager to have someone to love.

"Not mine," he said. Then he turned and headed toward her waiting SUV outside the hangar.

Ava and Oliver helped one of the flight crew members load the dog into another vehicle so he could be taken straight to the vet's office.

Oliver joined her by the SUV. "You handled that nicely."

"He's been through a lot and he still has a long way to go. Each disappointment is just another setback."

"Sounds as if you've been there."

"I went through a hard time when I got home, but I told you that."

"You skimmed over it, yes. Maybe if you told me more—"

"Not a good time to analyze me, Oliver."

"I'm not trying to analyze you," he said, his words for her only. "Just trying to understand you." His eyes holding hers, he added, "You just told Isaac not to give up. Like him, you survived and you've come a long way. But you're afraid to take that next step. I get that. I'm afraid, too."

"Let's go," she said, not liking how he seemed to understand her too well already. "I have more work to do."

Oliver walked around and got in the front seat, a frown deepening the fatigue that seemed to cloak him these days.

From the back seat, Isaac sent Ava a long stare through

the rearview mirror when she started the vehicle. Then he leaned forward and asked, "What's with you two, anyway?"

"We have no idea," she replied.

Isaac gave her that soft smile he kept hidden away. "Right."

Oliver shook his head and stared out the window.

What was with them? she wondered after she'd dropped Isaac off at his house.

Oliver must have been wondering the same thing because as soon as they were back on the road he asked, "What *is* going on with us?"

"Like I said, I have no idea."

But she did have an idea. A pretty good idea.

She was falling in love with Oliver Davison.

And that was the worst possible thing she could do.

"Can we go somewhere and talk?" Oliver asked Ava when they reached his car.

"No. I told you, I have work to do."

"You're finding work to do so you can avoid me."

"Isn't that the plan? To avoid each other?"

"It should be the plan, and yet even your immediate superior is throwing us together."

"No, he was forced to allow you to come along because you were hounding him about wanting to talk to me."

"Well, yes, I did do that."

Ava turned to face him, her hands still on the steering wheel. "Oliver, we need to take a break. The Red Rose Killer is after both of us, so let's keep him guessing by splitting up."

He knew she was right. "That's usually a good idea, but I worry about you."

Ava glanced around and then back to where his car

was parked a couple of spaces over. "And I worry about you, too." Pointing to his vehicle, she said, "I think you have a flat tire."

Pivoting, Oliver took in the sight of the deflated front tire on the driver's side. "How did that happen? It was fine when I got here earlier."

Getting out, he examined it and then kicked it. "Great, just what I needed today."

"We can change it," Ava said as she came around her SUV.

"I'll take care of it," he replied, aggravation getting the best of him. "But not until I'm sure you're safely back inside the building."

"We're right here," she said, checking all around them. "No one would dare mess with me here."

"Ava, someone has already messed with people here and they didn't live to tell about it, and yesterday, someone was hiding in the bushes listening to us."

At the hurt in her eyes, he grabbed her hand. "I'm so sorry. I shouldn't remind you of your friends. I know their murders are a big part of why you're so determined to find Boyd Sullivan."

She nodded and took a deep breath. "No, you don't need to remind me of that. Everyone I work with wants to bring in the Red Rose Killer. And since that's your goal, too, why don't we do what we started out doing? Work together."

Relief washed over Oliver. Finally, they could quit pushing each other away. "I can live with that."

Lowering her head, she leveled her gaze on him. "But there is one stipulation."

So much for relief and hope. "And what's that?"

"Nothing social. We show up here and work with the rest of the team. We compare notes and go over details.

We even go back into the woods and retrace our steps. Sullivan could still be out there, for all we know. Or he could have a bead on Turner Johnson."

"I don't like—"

Ava held up a hand. "I do my job, my way, same as I did before you showed up. And you do your job, your way."

She was asking too much. "I can't stop wanting to protect you, Ava."

"And I can't stop worrying about you," she replied. "But we keep those feelings compartmentalized for now."

"You mean, until this is over."

"Yes. No more dinners or forced excursions or coffee breaks." She stepped back. "Now, I'm going inside and you get that tire changed and get back to work."

"Bossy, too, aren't you?"

She didn't answer. Instead she stood her ground. "Can we agree?" she asked, her tone hopeful but firm. Was that a trace of regret he saw in her eyes?

"Do I have a choice?"

"This is the best solution for now," she said, turning to let Roscoe out of his kennel. "I'll see you later."

Oliver nodded but decided she couldn't stop him from watching her until she made it into the building.

When she reached the middle of the street, he heard the roar of a motorcycle and looked up in time to see a sleek black bike heading at full speed right toward Ava and Roscoe.

SEVENTEEN

Oliver didn't stop to think. Sprinting toward where Ava stood frozen, he called out, "Run."

But Ava appeared to be more worried about Roscoe. "Go," she ordered, her body shielding her partner. The K-9 did as he was told but he whirled and barked at Ava.

Oliver made it to her and shoved her with all his might. Ava went down, sliding across the pavement and twisting around while Oliver felt the impact of the big bike against his left thigh. Just enough impact to cause the high-powered machine to skid and slide before rolling sideways into the grass between the street and the sidewalk.

Oliver tried to stand, but his leg gave out. "Stop," he shouted as the driver managed to get up off the grass and jog away.

"I've got it," Ava called, but she winced and cried out. "Roscoe, find."

Glad for the chance, Roscoe barked and took off in a leap toward where the dark figure had headed.

Oliver grunted and tried to get to Ava. People started running out of the training yard, sirens echoed, dogs barked. Ava moaned and stood on shaky legs and moved toward him.

"Oliver?" She crumpled beside him and grabbed his hand.

"I'm okay," he said, the warmth of her hand touching his. But he also felt something else on her hand. Blood, sticky and wet from where she'd skidded onto the pavement. "You're hurt. I pushed you too hard."

"You saved my life," she replied, tears gathering like rain clouds in her eyes. "Oliver, are you all right?"

"Let us check," someone said from behind them.

"Her first," Oliver said.

And then he passed out.

Ava sat on an exam table in a tiny room at the base hospital ER, wondering what was going on with Oliver. He'd passed out and then someone had lifted her up onto a gurney and rushed her to the hospital. Now no one would tell her anything about Oliver or Roscoe and she was going to scream if she didn't hear soon.

Her hands had ointment and bandages on them and her knees were scraped, her uniform pants were torn and her whole body ached with bruises, but she was alive.

Oliver had put himself in harm's way to save her.

What if he didn't wake up? Had he hit his head when he'd gone down? It all happened so fast. The sound of a roaring motorcycle, Oliver's warning, Roscoe's fierce barking, and then the sound of a motorcycle skidding on the pavement.

She'd glanced up in a blur of confusion to see the driver dressed in all black—helmet, gloves, clothes, goggles.

Was it the same person who kept trying to shoot her and Oliver?

She didn't know. But whoever it was, they were getting closer and closer.

Too close.

Ava grabbed at the hospital gown around her and tried to slip off the table.

"Whoa, there."

Glancing up, she was ready to do battle with anyone trying to stop her. But it was Pastor Harmon, his hazel eyes bright with amusement. "Going somewhere, Senior Airman Esposito?"

Ava managed to get back up on the table, pulling the lightweight blanket after her. "I need to find out if my K-9 partner is okay and Special Agent Oliver Davison got hurt trying to protect me and…and…"

She stopped, very near tears. She refused to cry, even in front of the one man who could handle any woman's tears.

"Okay," Pastor Harmon said, his expression oscillating between pity and understanding, his neatly clipped sandy-brown hair combed into place. "Okay, why don't you rest and I'll get you some answers, how about that?"

Ava sniffed. "Thank you, Pastor. And thanks for stopping by, too. Have you heard anything?"

"I just got here," he said, calm as always. "I do know the doctors are with your special agent. Something about X-rays, but don't quote me on that."

"X-rays," Ava said, her heart bursting with too many emotions. "That could mean a lot of different things."

"Yes, and since I'm not a doctor, let's not get all worried about that right now." He patted her hand. "Is there anything I can do for you, Ava?"

"You mean, besides the usual?"

"Oh, I'm praying for all of you, yes. Anything else? A drink or another blanket?"

"No," she replied, grateful for his calming presence. "But you did mention finding out about Roscoe."

"I'm on it," the pastor replied. "I'll track down someone who looks official."

"Thank you," Ava said, suddenly exhausted.

She was dozing off when the door opened again and Vanessa Gomez came in, her smile bright. "Ava, are you stirring up trouble with a man of God?"

"No one will tell me anything," Ava said, her suspicious mind going into overdrive. Was the nurse here to check on her, or snuff her out for good? Ava reminded herself there was a guard outside her door. Vanessa had obviously been cleared and they were obviously watching.

Vanessa gave her an overall appraisal. "I came in to tell you that you're okay. I'm on duty, but on my break, and since I'm not your regular duty nurse, I can't do anything too official, but I thought I'd sit with you while you wait to hear on Special Agent Davison."

"Can you tell me anything?" Ava asked, all the while checking for sharp needles or deadly chloroform. But all she saw was a tired nurse who seemed to want to make her feel better.

Could Vanessa be that good at hiding her connections to Boyd Sullivan? Or had she been the one on that motorcycle earlier? Ava said she was on break, so that meant she'd been here at the hospital all day.

"You look perplexed," Vanessa said. "I'm sure Oliver will be just fine. From what I heard, he's bruised badly on one hip and suffered a few contusions on his face and left arm. The X-ray is probably to make sure nothing's broken."

"Is that all you know?" Ava asked, impatient. "Did they catch the driver?"

Vanessa sighed. "I'm sorry, I don't know anything. I

shouldn't have told you that much, but Pastor Harmon felt a revolt might be coming."

"He did catch me trying to get out of here."

"Why don't you just rest until someone can escort you home?"

"Where is Roscoe?" Ava asked, panic setting in.

A knock at the door brought her head up. Vanessa opened the door and saluted Captain Justin Blackwood and then excused herself. "I hope you feel better soon, Ava."

Ava nodded after saluting. "Thank you, Vanessa."

Captain Blackwood stared after the nurse. "Why was she here?"

"Checking on me and giving me a report, sort of," Ava admitted. "She said she was on break and the guard cleared her to enter."

"I see." Justin held his thoughts close to his chest, too. "I'll verify that."

Maybe they were both being too suspicious, but lately Ava had to go on the notion that anyone could be guilty.

"Roscoe is safe," the blue-eyed captain said in his no-nonsense way. "He's with Lila Fields."

"Lila's a great trainer, sir. I'm glad to hear Roscoe's in good hands."

Lila was new to the training program and a single mother to a toddler daughter. Ava had often chatted with her in the break room.

"Yes, she's going to be an asset to us," Justin replied. "Listen, the driver of the bike managed to slip over a fence. We've got the base on lockdown but so far no sign of them. We did find one scrape of black material, probably from their pants. Sent it to the crime lab to be tested for DNA evidence."

"That's something." Ava wondered if they'd find anything at all. "But these people have managed to cover their tracks over and over. If we can't find the driver, that means it's someone who knows this base and knows where to hide."

"I agree and we're on it," Justin replied. "Special Agent Davison is okay, Ava. Badly bruised hip and left leg so he'll be out of commission for a few days. Which means if you're up to it, we'll need you back out there looking around."

"I'll be fine, sir. When can I go home?"

"That's up to the doctors," Justin replied. "I'm sure you'll hear soon, but…if you don't get cleared for duty you'll have to accept that, understood?"

"Yes, sir."

Ava talked to the captain awhile longer, going over the few details she remembered. "I don't know if the driver was male or female. It happened so quickly. But it could have been the same figure we've seen in the woods and, possibly, in San Antonio."

"You relax and we'll keep searching," Justin said. "Roscoe tried his best but that fence got between him and the runner. We lost the scent about four blocks over near the main entryway. Whoever it is left the base somehow."

Feeling her superior's frustrations, Ava waited for Captain Blackwood to leave and then managed to get dressed in her torn uniform again. By the time the ER doctor came in to release her, she was ready to go.

But she wasn't going anywhere until she talked to Oliver.

Oliver grunted and kicked his good leg. "I can't stay here overnight. I need to be out there."

"You're injured," ER doctor Trevor Knight repeated to him, his blue eyes full of authority. "You came close to a hip fracture. You can barely walk right now, let alone chase after a killer. And we need to watch that head wound, too."

"They tried to run down Ava," Oliver said, realizing too late he'd addressed her by her first name and not her rank. But Oliver was beyond caring about protocol right now.

"I know, but you saved her and she's okay. In fact, I just left her. I released her to go home."

"Not without me," Oliver said, trying to turn and stand. But the pain that shot down his leg made him break out into a cold sweat. "Not without me," he said on a weaker note.

Trevor pinned Oliver with a doctor's glare. "You do realize that Senior Airman Esposito is well trained and more than qualified to take care of herself, right?"

"Yes, I'm well aware of that fact," Oliver said, his head throbbing like a machine gun. "But thank you and everyone else for reminding me."

"Why don't you rest," Trevor suggested. "That's the best thing you can do right now. If you get out there and can't protect your…friend, then she'll have to take care of herself and you."

Oliver finally caved, knowing the doc was right. But he still worried about Ava. Closing his eyes, he said a prayer for protection. Then he lay there thinking about how much she'd come to mean to him over these last couple of weeks.

He was beginning to think he might be in love with Ava.

And he was probably the last person involved in this case to realize that.

Ava had been trained to be as quiet as possible while tracking for lost military personnel or trying to bring home a wounded soldier. Using those same tactics now, she found Oliver's room and quietly opened the door.

He was asleep, his frown evidence that he wasn't happy to be here either. Walking gingerly since she was sore all over, she made it to the bed and stared down at him. She didn't want to love the man, and yet her heart seemed to swell with something she'd never felt before, not even with Julian.

Had Julian been a crush or a distraction during a horrible time in theater? Or would she always hold him dear as her first true love?

Maybe both, but standing here now, she felt something strong and solid and unflappable for the man before her. Oliver was the real deal.

She wanted to know everything about him. How he'd handled growing up in New York State, where he'd gone to school, his first crush, his first time feeling broken-hearted and alone. What he'd seen and done out there in the tough world of the FBI.

And she wanted to share the intimate details of her life with him. Growing up without a lot of hope and no money to provide that hope, joining the air force so she could travel and finish her education and make something of herself. Almost dying while she watched the man she loved die right before her eyes. Changing in midstride from becoming a pilot to becoming a K-9 handler and a member of the Working Dog program. She wanted to share all of that with Oliver.

So she took his hand and held it tight and prayed to God to give them the strength and resources they needed to find the Red Rose Killer and his accomplice.

"We won't stop fighting," she whispered. And then she leaned down and kissed him. "I won't stop fighting for you, and soon we'll get past all of this."

Oliver sighed in his sleep. She turned to go, not wanting to wake him. But he called out, "Hey, did I hear you talking to me? Or was that a dream?"

Ava turned and headed back to the bed. "No dream. But you need to rest, okay?"

"What about you?"

"I'm okay," she said, his husky voice strumming across her soul. She wanted to say so many things, but now was not the time. She needed to get back out there. "I'll check back with you later," she said.

Oliver reached out a hand to touch her sleeve. "Be careful."

"Always."

She'd do her job, but she'd also try very hard to hold back on her growing feelings for Oliver. It was too dangerous to let her heart take over when she needed her head in the game.

EIGHTEEN

Two days later, frustration colored Oliver's words. He was obviously still in a lot of pain, and he'd been quiet. Too quiet. "Neither of these women do anything but work, shop at the BX and go straight home. You'd think they'd have social lives, at least."

Ava's disappointment matched Oliver's aggravation. Over the last couple of days, they'd set up surveillance on Vanessa Gomez and Yvette Crenville, but so far they'd heard nothing out of the ordinary from the people they'd had watching the two women. They didn't have enough evidence to delve into phone records or bank accounts at this point and no probable cause to get a warrant.

"Vanessa goes to church," she said. "Can't say the same for Yvette, but the woman sure loves to jog around the base and pay occasional surprise visits to all the refrigerators in the break rooms to fuss at us about our unhealthy eating habits."

"Or to spy," he retorted as he hobbled to the coffee pot in the training center lounge. "She's probably placed a bug in here somewhere." Then he grunted and leaned on the table. "She could easily be the Anonymous Blogger since she pops up everywhere."

"I'm liking her more and more as Sullivan's accomplice," Ava admitted. "But we have no proof. The worst we have on Yvette is that one of our people saw her wolfing down a huge chocolate bar while sitting on her front steps. And that's not a crime, or most women I know would be in jail."

Oliver shook his head at that. "And when we interviewed her months ago, she said she hated Sullivan and never wanted to see him again. Which is also not a crime."

"They did have a very public breakup from what I've heard," Ava said. "But she seemed worried when I saw her jogging the other morning. He could easily turn on her if she doesn't do his bidding."

She almost mentioned the creepy feeling Yvette had given her, but she'd reported the encounter to her superiors, so she wouldn't add to his worries now. His bruised leg was better, but he was grumpy and he worked on shouting orders over the phone, since he couldn't work off steam in the exercise room yet.

But Ava got the impression that something was bothering him beyond this investigation. The tension between them seemed to be getting worse instead of better, and she didn't want any rumors to get back to that annoying blogger.

Ava thought about Yvette's habit of jogging day and night. "It would be easy to go out and purposely be seen and then slip off the jogging trail, throw on some hidden clothes and do her dirty deeds. But that's a stretch."

"We don't discount any scenario. Still waiting on the footage from the outdoor superstores near San Antonio, too," Oliver reminded Ava. "They gave us a hard time at first, but now they're allowing one of my agents to go through sales receipts and look at surveillance footage. But that could take a while."

"We're not getting anywhere now," Ava replied. "Maybe that will bring us something."

She rubbed her eyes to get what felt like sawdust out of them. They'd been holed up here all day, waiting to hear what the lab found out about the scrap of material the motorcycle rider had left behind. If there was any trace of DNA, it could help them. Now she watched Oliver grit his teeth as he tried to pretend he was fine.

"I'm better," Oliver said, as if reading her thoughts.

"I know that," she replied.

"Then stop looking at me like that. Sympathy is beautiful in your eyes, but I don't need pity, Ava. I need to get back out there."

"You're still not able to walk very well," she pointed out. And he refused to take any pain pills. Stubborn man that he was. "Maybe you should do some of the stretches the physical therapist suggested."

"The more I move, the less pain I'll be in," he said with a grimace. "And that means I'm capable of walking around in the woods."

"But you can't run, Oliver."

"I don't plan on running. I can still use a weapon."

"Why don't we get out of here for a while?" she said. "It's a nice fall day. We can grab some food and find a bench, get some sun."

"Chase a bad guy," he added, smiling. "That sounds like a good idea."

"Chasing the bad buy or getting out of here?"

"Both."

Ava called to Roscoe and soon they were in her SUV, driving toward the Winged Java. It seemed to be their place, and since everyone had noticed them hanging out together and working together, no one dared tease them or question when they left the training center headquarters. Except to warn them to be vigilant, of course.

"We'll raise eyebrows," Oliver said, favoring his left leg while he sat back in his seat.

"We are way past raising eyebrows," Ava replied. "But you know, a lot of people around me have started dating, and some are getting engaged and even getting married. That seems to be in the air around here in spite of the horrible situation that brought them together."

At his silence, she glanced over at him. "Not that I'm hinting or anything." Then she let out a groan. "Never mind."

Oliver finally looked over at her. "It's not what you think."

"Oh, really? Lately, you've been clamming up like a tortoise. Isn't that a typical man thing?"

"Did you just call me a tortoise?"

"You act like one sometimes."

"Ava, I'm trying to do my job, same as you. I would have thought you'd be glad I'm staying quiet these days." He shrugged. "I haven't been around a woman this much since—"

"Since Madison," she finished, feeling as low as a person could sink. "I'm sorry. So sorry. I must remind you of her death and the Red Rose Killer whenever we're together."

"I didn't mean it that way." He looked even more aggravated, so she decided to drop that thread of conversation.

She stopped the SUV in the café parking lot and her cell went off as she was reaching for the door handle.

Oliver's buzzed at the same time.

"Esposito."

"Davison."

As soon as they answered, Ava listened on her line to Westley's voice, her eyes on Oliver. "Yes, sir, we'll be right there."

Oliver listened and then said into the phone, "Hey, somebody needs to grab my FBI jacket, my Kevlar vest and my weapon out of the locker you assigned me."

Then they both put away their phones.

"The motorcycle was stolen but the DNA on the torn fabric matches Boyd Sullivan," she said, knowing Oliver had just heard the same. "I sure thought that person could have been a woman."

"Maybe it was a woman but she borrowed Sullivan's sweatpants," Oliver said. "They've had sightings in the woods again. Let's get going."

"No," Ava said, giving Oliver one of her not-happy stares. "You can't go on this search."

"Yes, I can," he replied, adrenaline giving him a boost of confidence. "Ava, I have to be in on this. For a lot of reasons. The man tried to kill you."

"I'm fine," she said, her eyes on the highway leading to the reserve. "My equipment is in the back and I'm ready to go."

"You're still bruised, too."

She shot him a frown. "And you're still limping."

"You can't take me home or back to the K-9 center. We don't have time."

"Okay, all right." She beat a hand against the wheel. "But you have to stay near this vehicle, understood?"

He slanted a stern stare her way. "I don't take orders from you."

"Oliver, please," she said. "I thought I'd lost you the other day when I saw that motorcycle hit you."

"Did that make you care?"

"You know I care, even if you don't make it easy. As I said, I thought they'd killed you."

"But they didn't. I'm hard to get rid of. I'll be okay. I'll do a ride along with one of the OSI people or Security Forces."

She gave him another headstrong stare but didn't argue anymore. They made it to the command post set up half a mile from the opening trail into the woods. All around, officers from the Office of Special Investigations, Security Forces and the K-9 unit were stalking through the woods. Sullivan could be long gone by now.

"Here we go again," Ava said. "We've got a few hours before dark."

"Then let's get cracking."

He watched as Ava put on her protective gear and strapped on her weapons. After checking her knapsack, she turned to Roscoe. "Ready, boy."

Oliver worried about her, too, but he knew better than to voice that concern. She was independent and strong and not to be reasoned with when she was on a search.

But he wasn't about to sit this one out. So he got out of the vehicle with a shrug and gritted his teeth. "I can't sit here when the action is out there."

Surprisingly Ava didn't push back. Her mind was no doubt already on what they might find in those woods.

Captain Justin Blackwood and Master Sergeant Caleb Streeter met them as they walked up the narrow strip of road.

"Hey," Caleb said. He gave Oliver the once-over. "Are you ready for this?"

"I walked about a half mile just now," Oliver said, wishing they'd all quit worrying about him. "I'm good. Where's my gear?"

Chad Watson, now completely recovered from his

gunshot wound, jogged up and helped Oliver get on his bulletproof vest and check his weapon. "We gotta stop meeting like this, Special Agent Davison."

"I couldn't agree more," Oliver said, thanking the Security Forces officer.

Ian Steffen from the Office of Special Investigations stalked up. "I just got word that someone tried to break into the Johnson house."

Oliver met Ava's apprehensive gaze. "Was Turner home?" he asked Ian. "Is the boy okay?"

"I'm waiting to hear," Ian replied. "We've sent a squad to check." He scrolled his phone. "We've had eyes on the boy since the incident out here so we expected this."

"That could be a diversion," Oliver said, "to throw us off."

"Yes, I did consider that," Ian responded.

His phone buzzed. Listening, he said, "I see. I'll alert the necessary people."

Ian ended the call and looked at Ava and Oliver, his eyes narrowed.

"Someone has taken the boy."

Oliver called the Security Forces officer who'd responded to the 911 alert at the colonel's home.

"Suspect tried to get in through a side door but was seen in the backyard," the officer explained. "Parents alerted our people. The kid was playing in his fort but tried to escape. Last Mrs. Johnson saw, someone dressed in dark clothing was carrying her son toward the woods behind the house. They held a gun on the boy and told her to back off."

"How did they get past our guards?"

"Found one knocked out and the other one is missing."

"I'm coming there myself," Oliver said, ending the call.

Caleb Streeter hurried toward Oliver. "I think I know why someone went after the boy, Special Agent."

"What now?" Oliver asked, his leg protesting each step.

"Our Anonymous Blogger leaked earlier today that Security Forces and the FDI were considering a lineup so that Turner Johnson could identify the woman he saw with the Red Rose Killer."

"What?" Oliver stomped his foot and then moaned. "That's classified."

Ava put a hand to her mouth. "Oh, no. So that's why they took Turner. Oliver, they could kill him."

"I know," he said. He went into action, making calls, giving orders, stomping and pacing. "I know," he said again after he'd done all he could do from there. "Let's go."

"I'll radio the others."

A few minutes later, they were back in her SUV. "We can have Roscoe search the house, at least. Maybe find us a trail. I can't believe this is happening again, and all because that blogger sent out misinformation."

Oliver nodded, his bruised leg on fire with pain, his stomach churning.

"We have to find the person who's been somehow listening to all of us and leaking things that cause everyone to be in danger," he said. "And we have to find Turner. Before it's too late."

NINETEEN

Colonel Johnson's home was stately and well maintained, the lush yard sloping down to a small stream that ran along the property. Tall cottonwoods and oaks lined the area near the woods while the landscaping around the house contained various shade trees and blooming shrubs. A wooden fence enclosed the backyard and a chain-link fence could be seen finishing out the enclosure about fifty feet beyond the wooded area and stream.

A good place to hold a picnic.

Also a good place for an intruder to lurk and wait.

"But we have security," Marilyn Johnson kept saying, the shock of her son missing yet again taking its toll on the woman. "How could this happen? We were so careful."

Ava held the woman's shaking hand. "Mrs. Johnson, can you tell me why Turner was out there all alone?"

"It's my fault, isn't it?" the distraught woman said, tears forming in her eyes. "He was here with me but he wanted to go outside. I got up to check on dinner and told him I'd be right back and…he'd slipped out ahead of me. I heard Stormy barking and then I ran out the door."

"So he was playing in the fort and you called to him?"

"I saw him climbing down from his little fort. Stormy

kept barking." Marilyn glanced toward where the colonel was talking to Oliver. "Yes, and he came running when I called but that person jumped out of nowhere and grabbed him and held a gun on him. Told me to stay back or they'd kill my son. Stormy tried to stop it, but the intruder kicked him and then took Turner toward the stream. He must have cut the fence."

"What did this person look like? What was this person wearing?"

"I told the others already. All black, sunshades, a dark hat, long sleeves, bulky pants. All dark and unrecognizable. I can't say who I saw."

She put her hands to her ears. "I can still hear Turner screaming and Stormy barking. Why can't you people do your jobs and find this murderer?"

Hearing his name, Stormy came running. The little dog was okay, thankfully. But Ava's worries centered on Turner.

"We'll find him," Ava said, nodding to Oliver.

The sooner they got out there, the better things would be. The chain-link fence had been cut in the far back right corner. But she wouldn't burden Mrs. Johnson with the details right now.

Oliver hurried to her. "No sign of anyone down by the stream, but we found footprints leading due west."

"I'm not waiting around," Ava said. "I'm going after Turner."

"I'm with you," Oliver replied. "I've got a team here from our Bureau already setting up phone monitors and they know the drill. They'll let us know if they receive any demands." Then he looked grim. "Not that I expect any ransom demands. They want to silence the boy."

"This has to be Sullivan or his accomplice. He has to

know we'll track him," Ava said, her mind reeling with every possible scenario.

"Yes, that's exactly what he expects, but we're going to do it differently this time."

"What do you mean?"

Oliver leaned close. "I called Heidi Jenks and told her to head to the reserve and make a big to-do, taking pictures and interviewing people. The paper can post to its website immediately. And so can the televison reporters who'll hear this on their scanners and show up out there."

"But—" Ava stopped short. "But we won't be there."

"Exactly. Just you, me and Roscoe will be out in *these* woods. Less of a chance he'll know we're here."

"But if he's watching the house?"

"We came in a side door and all of the drapes are closed. He won't even know we're here. All he can see is the guard at the back door." He shrugged. "Besides, if he's smart, he's long gone by now. Bad for us but that's how he'd do it. Get the kid away and send all of us scattering like rats to find him."

"Okay, and what if he's already left the area? He might not take Turner to the woods. He might take him across state lines."

"He's an hour or so out, but we can get a fresh track on him. He'd wait until full dark to leave the area or he could be seen, so we have a window of opportunity."

"Do you think he'll hurt Turner?"

Oliver put a hand on her arm and looked into her eyes. "We don't know if it's him." But yes, he knew Sullivan would do whatever he had to do to survive. And he suspected Ava knew that, too.

She nodded. "This could be a trap, but we have to try to save Turner."

* * *

After they'd alerted Oliver's agents to the plan, Ava and Oliver took Roscoe and made their way down the street to the higher level of the stream. They'd backtrack to this spot and hope Roscoe would pick up a scent, since Oliver was pretty sure Sullivan or possibly his accomplice had followed the stream to the edge of the Johnson property and managed to get past the security cameras and knock out one of the guards. The other guard had come running when he heard the screams and the barking, but he'd been shot in the shoulder. Thankfully both guards were okay.

Oliver wanted to get out there and search.

The coming dusk was quiet, a crisp fall breeze hitting them as they moved through the heavy foliage. Oliver hung back and let Ava and Roscoe do their job. She had let the dog sniff one of Turner's T-shirts and he took off toward the stream almost immediately.

Oliver moved slowly but he didn't complain. No need to whine now and he had to stay alert, so pain pills were out of the question.

"How are you doing?" Ava said on a low whisper as they moved through the decayed leaves.

"I'm either better or too numb to care," he admitted. "Adrenaline is a good drug, you know."

"Until you come down from it."

"I'll be okay, Ava. I've been worse off than this."

She didn't respond to that. If they were to have any type of relationship, she had to accept the bad with the good. Oliver didn't know if she'd ever step over that line. She'd seen someone she loved die in a horrible place and in a horrible way. She was afraid to open her heart up to that kind of pain again.

He certainly understood that notion. The realization

that he might be falling for her had sobered him and left him dazed and confused. Oliver wasn't sure how to handle all the emotions this woman brought out in him.

It wasn't too late to walk away and they both knew it.

He wanted the Red Rose Killer and his dangerous accomplice to be captured and put away for good this time. Taking a child had ratchetted things up a notch. Oliver prayed they could save Turner and find a way to keep him safe.

After that, he'd think about the woman he was falling in love with.

They walked in silence for a few minutes, Roscoe leading them along the rocky streambed. They rounded a curve where the water rushed and gurgled.

"This leads to the river," Ava said. "That makes sense since the river's not that far from here."

Roscoe alerted as the creek grew deeper.

Oliver felt the hair on the back of his neck rising. "It could be showtime."

"If he's picking up a scent, that means they haven't crossed the water yet," Ava said. "Maybe we should split up to be sure?"

Oliver shook his head. "Not a good idea."

"We can stay close but I'm going up ahead with Roscoc."

Oliver stared at her for a minute. "If something happens one of us needs to be able to call for backup."

"Yes."

He finally agreed to move higher up along the shore so he could explore and keep his eyes on her and the K-9.

Between the moonlight and their muted flashlights, he should be able to watch their backs. "I can send out an SOS over the radio at any time," he said.

"Same here," Ava replied, glancing ahead.

Oliver nodded. "Be careful."

Ava smiled and signaled Roscoe with a silent command to go. Then they took off, following the water downhill.

Oliver said a prayer for all of them.

Roscoe emitted low, soft growls. Something was happening up ahead. Ava gave the silent signal to "Find" as they carefully moved forward, her night goggles showing them the way.

They reached an outcropping of rocks where the water grew swift. Roscoe stopped and looked back at Ava.

"What's up?" she asked, wondering what the dog had smelled or heard.

Then she heard a sound. A sob.

Ava's heartbeat accelerated. "Turner?"

A dark figure stepped out from the trees. Roscoe growled low. Ava saw why the dog had remained still.

The dark figure was holding Turner Johnson.

"Let him go," Ava said, drawing her weapon.

The kidnapper shoved the boy forward, a gun at his back. "I will. But I want you to take his place. So if you try anything stupid, such as commanding that dog to attack me, I'll have to take the boy instead. Do you understand?"

Ava nodded, her eyes on Turner. "Turner, are you okay?"

The boy bobbed his head, his eyes wide, his sobs gone now. "She's been singing to me but…I don't like her."

She. The woman had disguised her voice somehow, but Turner obviously knew his captor was female. And he was smart enough to blurt that out.

Ava didn't respond or react. "I'll go with you and I'll send my dog away with the boy."

"That would work."

"Why do you want me?" Ava asked, stalling, wondering where Oliver had gone.

Or worse, what had happened to him.

Oliver heard voices a few yards ahead. He'd spotted some knocked-down shrubs and undergrowth, footsteps evident in the indentions. He'd only stopped for a couple of minutes.

Then he heard another noise not far from where he was standing. He whirled, his gun raised, and hit his foot on a protruding stone. He stumbled and fell hard, sliding about five feet down to the bank of the stream. Pain shot through his body but he managed to get up. Then he heard more voices echoing through the woods.

Oliver held on to rocks and bushes, saplings and trees, moving along the streambed so he could follow the voices.

They were moving toward the river. And the river wasn't far from where the woods behind the base picked back up. The river ran through the reserve from northwest to southeast. Sullivan and his accomplice could have been using the river to make their getaways all this time.

Oliver stopped to get his breath, the pain in his left leg throbbing like fire-tipped hammers. Then he heard someone rushing through the woods.

Managing to drop behind an old log, Oliver waited.

"C'mon, Roscoe," he heard someone saying. "You got to get me out of here."

Turner?

Lifting up his head, Oliver saw the boy, wet and dirty, holding on to Roscoe's leash. Where was Ava?

"Why are you doing this?" Ava asked, biding her time until she could make a break for it.

She'd given Roscoe the order to "Go Back" and then she'd handed the leash to Turner. Roscoe would take the boy home, she hoped. The dog had a special bond with Turner, having guarded him on that ledge and knowing his scent so well. Roscoe would know what to do.

The woman shoving her ahead on the path made it impossible for Ava to see who she really was. She'd disguised her voice and her face and she wore several layers of clothing. She used no perfume, covered her hands and face. She had to be sweating inside all that gear.

"Talk to me," Ava said, checking their location, the moonlight showing her they were headed toward the river. "Why did you take Turner?"

"He knows too much," came the muffled reply. "And so do you."

"So you're going to kill me?"

"Yes. And my boyfriend will take care of the boy."

Ava's heart lurched at that comment. The woman had tricked her. Now they'd kill both the boy and her and then they'd find Oliver. Or maybe that's why he hadn't found her.

What if Oliver was already dead?

His leg was going to give out.

Oliver stood up, hoping he wouldn't scare the boy and the K-9. "Hey, Turner, it's Agent Davison."

The boy whirled, his hand holding on to the leash. "FBI?"

"Yes, FBI," Oliver called. "We've been looking for you. Are you okay?"

The boy tried to pull Roscoe back. "I'm fine now. Roscoe is supposed to be taking me home. He won't turn back."

"What happened to Ava—Airman Esposito?"

"She took her," Turner said, his voice trembling. "Like a swap."

Oliver's chest hurt and a new rush of adrenaline gave him the strength he needed. "You need to get to safety. I'm going to call for help and alert them you're on your way home, okay?"

Roscoe barked. Not a growling bark, but more of an alert that meant "We have to keep going."

"Okay," Turner said. "I'm scared they'll come back. Will Roscoe bite them?"

"Of course," Oliver said, hoping the dog would do just that. "Meantime, I'm right behind you. So don't be scared. We're calling for backup."

He'd get the boy safely home and then he'd find Ava.

He just prayed he wouldn't be too late.

Ava knew it was now or never. The closer they got to the river, the worse things would go for her. If they took her on a boat, they could easily kill her and toss her in the water. Her body would wash up downriver.

She couldn't let that happen.

"So how long have you and Boyd been an item?" she asked now, hoping to get the woman riled enough that she'd become distracted. Hoping she'd figure out who this really was. Because she was beginning to think this person definitely wasn't Vanessa Gomez or Yvette Crenville. Boyd Sullivan could have a new paramour from another town.

The woman huffed out a couple of breaths and then replied, "Off and on, years. Not that it's any of your business."

Ava bobbed her head. "No, not my business except that you keep trying to kill me."

The woman's next words chilled her to the bone. "You're the only one he's ever let live."

Ava saw an incline up ahead and hoped there would be a gully or ravine on the other side. So she worked on her strategy a little more. "You know, I did notice that. We all did. I think he has a soft spot for me. Is that why he sent you to do his dirty work?"

The woman shoved Ava hard, but Ava was ready. She pretended to trip, her body going slack as she slid down. When the woman came after her, she lifted a booted foot and shoved it into the woman's padded midsection. The woman let out scream, lost control of her weapon and went backward, her bulky clothing softening her slide down into the ravine.

Ava scooted up and took off back toward Turner's house, running for her life while she prayed that Turner and Oliver were both safe.

Oliver dragged himself through the woods toward Turner and Roscoe. When he heard footsteps approaching and someone commanding Roscoe to "Guard," he knew the cavalry had come.

Up ahead, flashlights shone on the path. Oliver waved and called out. "Agent Davison. Over here."

Caleb Streeter and Ian Steffen hurried up to Oliver, both armed to the teeth in tactical gear.

Oliver grabbed Caleb's arm. "Ava? I don't know where she is. She sent Roscoe back with the boy."

"Which way?" Ian asked.

"Down the stream, toward the river."

Oliver took a deep breath and then he passed out.

TWENTY

"I'm all right."

Oliver kept pushing at the paramedics who'd arrived to check both him and Turner.

"Take it easy," someone said. "Just a precaution."

"I can walk," Oliver said. "Now let me up."

One of the first responders glanced at Ian and Westley. Westley nodded. "It's your call, Special Agent."

"Yes, so let me get back out there so I can find Ava."

They had him on a stretcher in the Johnsons' driveway, but he slid off the stretcher. Turner was inside with his parents and Stormy.

"Is the boy okay?" Oliver asked as he tried to stand. Gritting his teeth, he favored his left leg but managed to hobble toward a waiting SUV.

"He has some cuts and bruises, but he's a real trooper. He said the woman didn't hurt him. She mostly cried and wished she didn't have to do this."

"Can he identify her?"

"I don't think so," Ian replied. "But he did wonder out loud if it was the same woman he'd heard in the woods."

"Makes sense to me," Oliver said. He began to study the maps spread out on the hood of the vehicle, a spotlight shining on them. "We started out here and followed the stream to the river. I stayed a few yards behind Ava and Roscoe to search up high on some of the bluffs. They needed quiet and I was watching out for them. I found evidence that someone had traveled that way—broken branches, trampled grass and footprints in the dirt."

He pointed to the area on the map. "I think whoever took the boy stopped here to rest and regroup. Or to wait for us to show up." He shook his head. "We thought we'd fooled Sullivan but he fooled us. He's not here and he's probably not in the woods on this side of the river. He's been crossing over to get back and forth."

Finishing, he pointed to where the stream merged with the river. "Right here. This should be the entry point."

Justin Blackwood came up and studied the map. "Call in Search-and-Rescue," he said. "We need a chopper and this time, we work around the clock and use every means we have to find Boyd Sullivan."

"And the mysterious woman who's helping him," Oliver said. "But my intent is to find Ava."

Ava was halfway back to the Johnsons' house when she heard a twig snapping up ahead. The woman had thrown her weapon into the woods, so Ava had no way of protecting herself. Sliding behind a rock, she waited, holding her breath.

Had the woman survived that fall?

Not knowing what had happened to Oliver and praying Turner had made it home with Roscoe, Ava closed her eyes and held her breath, her prayers centered on the three of them.

Please, Lord, let them be safe. Roscoe knows his job.

Then she opened her eyes and searched for a weapon. Any weapon. Finding a big, aged tree branch, Ava grabbed it and waited.

Then she heard a woof. A friendly woof.

"Roscoe?"

Another woof, followed by a shout. "Ava?"

Roscoe rushed up and danced around her, woofing a happy tune.

"Oliver?" She stood, the glare of a flashlight temporarily blinding her. Then she heard a chopper overhead. "What's going on?"

Oliver hurried toward her and Ava immediately saw the pain on his face. "Oliver, are you all right?"

"I am now," he said, hugging her close. "How about you?"

"I'm fine. She had me but I got away. I kicked her off into a ravine and I ran because I was so worried about Turner and Roscoe."

"Turner is safe and doing great. He gave us a lot of details, including how she let it slip that her friend would be angry with her for doing this, but she had to get back to the river to meet him."

"Did Turner recognize her?"

"No. But he thinks it's the same woman he saw and heard in the woods."

"What are we doing?" she asked as people surrounded them.

Tech Sergeant Linc Colson came jogging up, his rottweiler, Star, with him. "Someone spotted a man who looked like Boyd Sullivan at the boat launch on the east shore of the river. We're bringing in two choppers and one found a spot to land about a mile from here. Let's get back to the house and move out."

"Can you walk?" Ava asked Oliver.

"I'm fine," he said. "I had a little tumble earlier but… I just needed to find you. The medics fixed me up and I'm good to go."

"This is serious if they're bringing in the choppers."

"Ian, Westley and Justin all agree we need to ramp things up. The woman is a problem, but she's either a big distraction so Sullivan can get away or she's gone rogue and is out to do you and me in, regardless of what the killer wants. She wanted to shut Turner up, and she didn't care who else she had to kill."

"Yes, but I pushed and she's very jealous of Sullivan. She thinks he's got a thing for me since he let me live."

"You must have struck a chord somewhere in his sick head."

"Or he's out for revenge against you."

"We need to find that woman and get the real story."

Ava sighed. "Meanwhile, Sullivan could be anywhere."

"Yes, so we're calling in more people and we'll use the chopper's technology to zoom in on any movement in the woods."

"That didn't help before."

"Well, we'll try again. I'm bringing in more agents, too. We're going to search with more intention on the other side of the river. An all-out manhunt leaving no stone unturned."

"I think we should since he slipped away last time. He's obviously been using the river to escape. The land on the other side is denser than the reserve connected to the base. We ended the search there last time because we thought he'd left the area."

Ava held his hand and guided him along through the trail, Roscoe leading the way while flashlights shone on their path out.

Once the medics had checked her over and released her, she geared up, secured new weapons and got Roscoe ready for their chopper ride.

When they made it to the rendezvous point, Oliver

took her hand in his. "They won't let me get in the chopper with you. My leg is hurting and I'd slow you down. But I'll be in on the search. I'll be riding shotgun in a Jeep."

"I'll see you there," she said, wanting to kiss him.

"Stay safe," he whispered. Then he squeezed her hand. "Go."

Ava got out of the vehicle, giving him one last look before she hurried with Roscoe to the waiting helicopter.

"Okay, Roscoe, you know the drill."

Ava prepared both their harnesses and got ready to rappel down into the black hole of the dense thicket. It had been a while since she'd done such an urgent nighttime search. Using GPS and the infrared system, they'd spotted a lone figure darting from the river into the woods. They believed that figure had to be the Red Rose Killer.

Now Ava had her night vision goggles and she had Roscoe geared up, the V-ring ready to hook to his harness. His vest was Kevlar and had all kinds of gadgets she could use if necessary. Including a flashlight with a battery pack and a built-in GPS to help her keep track of him.

This search had escalated to priority status now that they had evidence that Sullivan was back in the area.

But they hadn't found the woman. Ava got word on the radio that they'd searched the spot where Ava and the suspect had fought and saw signs that indicated the woman had slid down to the stream.

But she was nowhere to be found.

Exhaustion warred with adrenaline throughout Ava's system.

The crew prepared for the mission and then Ava did one last check and gave them the thumbs-up.

The gunner stationed behind one of the two .50 caliber machine guns gave Ava a nod, making her think of Julian.

He'd want you to keep moving, keep doing what you do, keep loving life. He'd want you to love again.

With that thought in mind, she held Roscoe in front of her and let the crew members guide her partner and her down to the ground.

Oliver sat in the Jeep, watching.

He needed to be out there, but he didn't want to keep others from doing their jobs. The open Jeep could get him close, however. The driver sent the Jeep flying through the woods, taking mudholes and ravines with the ease of a fighter pilot. Oliver held on and gritted his teeth, his leg throbbing less since they'd given him a mild pain reliever.

When they found the rendezvous point with the chopper he watched in awe as Ava slipped to the ground, loaded with gear and wearing a helmet and night goggles, and then unhooked herself and Roscoe all in one efficient movement.

The Jeep hovered on the narrow, overgrown path, watching and waiting along with Security Forces, the K-9 team and OSI members.

They'd all spread out through the woods in several different directions. Oliver got reports from his agents and gave advice as needed.

But after an hour, they still had nothing.

When his cell rang, he sat up straight. "Davison."

"We got some feedback from the superstore surveillance, sir. A tall female dressed in black went to two different area stores and purchased camping and fishing supplies." The agent named the dates, times and locations. "Paid with cash."

"Description?" Oliver asked, his gaze scanning the woods.

"Negative. She wore sunshades and a big hat. Probably wearing a wig, too."

Oliver thought of all the times he and Ava had spotted Sullivan's accomplice. Always in heavy black, no matter the Texas heat. And always so covered, no one could pick her out of a lineup. No one except a scared little boy whose parents didn't want him to have to suffer any more horrors.

Oliver couldn't push them on that either.

He ended the call with little more of a lead than he'd had before. They had a scrap of material with Boyd Sullivan's DNA on it and footage of an unidentifiable woman buying the exact kind of supplies needed to survive in a hot, bug-infested Texas thicket. And the boy's report that he'd been nabbed by a man and a woman who vacillated over killing him or holding him for ransom.

He suspected either Boyd or the woman had tried to shoot Oliver and Ava in San Antonio, but he had no solid proof there. Not even on the bike the driver had abandoned. They had the make and model on that and even the store where it had been purchased. But the owner had reported the bike stolen the same night Oliver and Ava had been in San Antonio.

"I'm losing my touch," he mumbled, frustration making his head roar.

They had to get a break, and soon. The base and the entire Hill Country area were on high alert again.

When he heard a ruckus in the woods and several dogs barking, Oliver looked around for his driver. The guy was nowhere to be found. So Oliver hopped out and went around to the driver's seat of the old Jeep and started it up. He wasn't waiting around. He had to help Ava and her team.

The chopper reported two possible hostiles moving in opposite directions through the woods. One team went to the east and another one spread out across the perimeters of the forest, while Ava took Roscoe and headed toward the west, staying within sight and communicating through her earbuds.

Roscoe alerted about a half mile deep into the woods. Ava had broken away from the others, letting her partner do his job. The foliage and undergrowth was so thick Ava had spurs and sharp nettles coating the legs of her camo pants. Her boots were dusty and caked with dirt and old mud. And the bugs were out to do her in, finding every bit of uncovered flesh despite the bug spray she'd hosed down with earlier.

But now Roscoe was definitely on a scent. The big dog moved with a tenacious zest up and down the hills and crevices. Then Roscoe stopped and pawed at something in the dirt before turning back to Ava.

She hurried over and bent down.

Another headband. This one solid black and dirty.

"Good boy," Ava said, lifting the headband with a stick to drop it into a small evidence bag. Then she put the bag into one of the many pockets attached to her uniform jacket.

"Go," she told Roscoe. "Find." If he had a scent from the Buff, maybe, just maybe, they'd find the mysterious woman and maybe, just maybe, she'd lead them to Boyd Sullivan.

Other dogs started barking off in the distance. The woods came alive with action. Roscoe sniffed the air and the forest floor and then took off toward the west.

They rounded a curve where a well-beaten path brought her to a hidden stream by a wide-mouth cave.

Ava spotted a camp just inside the big cave. She could see where a fire had burned, several empty cans lying there. There was water nearby and a roomy, almost hidden, shelter, two things someone on the run would need.

I think we've found his lair.

At last.

"Good job," she told Roscoe on a low whisper. "Good find."

Ava crept around the side of the rocky cave, hoping to wait for Sullivan or his accomplice to emerge. But if they'd heard the dogs, they'd be on the run again by now. Didn't he know that sooner or later they'd corner him in the woods?

She studied the cave through her night goggles. No movement. But it could go deep into the terrain and, just as she and Oliver had suspected, the cave could open up near the fence that protected Canyon Air Force Base. Ava stepped forward for a better scan.

Roscoe growled low and gave her a warning, but too late, she whirled. And heard the click of a gun in the darkness.

"At last, we meet again," the unseen gunman said, his voice lifting out over the woods in a disembodied echo. "I've given you so many chances to live, hoping that you'd leave me alone or that possibly we might even become close."

Ava tried not to flinch. "I'm here now. What do you want with me?"

Roscoe barked, loud and angry, sensing the danger and the evil. The roar of the choppers flying off in the distance gave her hope.

He moved close but stayed behind some heavy undergrowth. "Call off that mutt and turn off your radio, or our first date will end very quickly."

Ava commanded Roscoe. "Quiet. Stay." Then she switched off her only means of contact, took a breath and tried to focus on ending this. "What do you want?"

"I want you to come with me," he said. "My former

ally has suddenly deserted me and it's just so lonely in these woods."

"Did you kill her because she disobeyed you?"

"Not yet. I told her to back off. Too bad she didn't listen. Taking the boy was a bad mistake, her way of trying to get my attention. But it did bring you to me."

Ava swallowed the bile rising in her throat, not sure if she believed him or not, but very sure he would kill the woman who'd gone against his wishes. "That's too bad about your friend. She really wanted me out of the way. Tried to shoot me several times, but she's not a very good shot."

"I know. Tedious, really." He moved closer so she could finally see him, but he was covered in camo and had his face covered with a dark bandana. Holding a handgun aimed at her, he said, "Tell your dog to stay and then carefully clear your weapons out and drop them by the dog. Then you and I can go for a stroll in the moonlight."

Ava did as he asked, her prayers centered on surviving. She had no other choice. The others would find her. And meantime, she planned to do everything in her power to stop this man from killing again.

When she reached into her pocket, she felt something she'd forgotten she'd put there. The black headband Roscoe had found earlier. Making a production of slowly dropping her handgun and the extra magazines, she managed to loop the wide black band over her wrist.

Dropping that down with her weapons, she hoped it would be a sign that she'd been here and that she'd been taken by the Red Rose Killer. Taking one last glance at Roscoe, she gave him a loving stare, then started to walk in front of the gunman.

Find us, boy. Show them that you're never wrong.

TWENTY-ONE

"What do you mean, you don't know where she is?"

Oliver took off his FBI cap and ran a hand over his damp hair, his frown so rigid his temple throbbed in protest.

"She's gone off grid," K-9 handler Lieutenant Nick Donovan said. "No communication for the last thirty minutes."

"That's not good," Oliver said. "Ava knows not to do that. Where's Roscoe?"

"We were about to go search for both of them," Justin Blackwood told Oliver. "So either hop a ride or stay behind, but we're wasting time."

"I'm going."

Oliver limped to an off-road four-wheeler and got in the back seat since the extra front seat was occupied by a K-9 bloodhound. The pain running up and down his spine and hip was excruciating, but he had to find Ava. Something wasn't right.

"I should never have left her," he said to Nick. "I knew better."

"Hey, man, we've all been right here. She got a scent and she took off. It's what we do. We weren't that far behind."

"Someone should have stayed with her. Where's

Buster?" He wondered what had detained the burly Security Forces member.

"On another case but he's trying to get here," Nick replied over the noise of the ATV's motor. "We'll find her, Oliver. Just stay cool and get your head back into this."

Oliver knew his friend was right, so he took a deep breath and asked for updates. After Nick brought him up to speed, he checked in with his agents, relieved that they'd found signs of a campsite and had gathered what few items they could for evidence.

"The choppers spotted someone running toward the river and the dogs went into action when we advanced toward that area," Nick explained. "We found a dirty black hoodie—extra large—a pair of nylon jogging pants and some muddy black tennis shoes. The items were scattered, so the dogs were going wild."

"But you didn't find the person?"

"Nope. Either swam across the river or managed to throw off the scent enough to get away. One of your agents heard a motor cranking up, but we lost the scent in a clearing across the stream."

"And then you heard more barking?"

"Yes. And we realized Ava wasn't checking in."

Nick pulled the ATV up to a clearing and ordered his partner, Annie, down. "This is the last spot where we heard from her. She was onto something."

They got off the ATV and stalked quietly through the dark, low-beam flashlights leading the way. Nick clipped on his night goggles. They'd gone a few hundred yards, finding broken twigs and limbs here and there, when they heard a low growl.

"That could be Roscoe," Oliver whispered, hurrying past Nick and Annie. Annie's ear twitched in anticipation.

They came up on an open area. "Cave," he whispered to Nick.

Ava must have found a cave, and from the looks of it, it was the Red Rose Killer's hideout. Almost exactly like the one Oliver had spotted days ago on the other side of the river.

But this one was in a hidden spot in the middle of a deserted wilderness area that few humans ever saw.

And sitting in front of that cave, guarding what looked like a pile of weapons and equipment, Roscoe stared up at them with hope in his doleful eyes. Then he touched a paw to something lying amid the things Ava had left behind.

A dirty black headband. A Buff, Ava had called these things. Roscoe must have alerted on this. But Ava had left it as a sign, a big clue.

"This isn't Ava's." Oliver looked at Nick and then grabbed one of the weapons from the ground. "He took her. The Red Rose Killer took Ava. But she left something behind so we can find her."

He moved behind her, poking the gun at her ribs each time she tried to stop or turn to face him.

Ava kept her breathing steady to keep her nerves calm. "You know they're out here searching for you, right?"

"What else is new?" Boyd Sullivan asked with a harsh laugh.

"And you know that if anything happens to me, they will find you?"

"They haven't so far. It's really laughable how easy it is to get the jump on the whole Security Forces section. I might have flunked basic, but I know more about this base than any of you imbeciles."

Trying again while she ignored that bait, she asked, "Why are you so fixated on me?"

He stopped and yanked her back. "Isn't that obvious? *He* loves you. He didn't love Madison but he loves you. I want him to suffer."

Ava decided Sullivan's logic was skewed. "But you killed her. You killed the woman you loved."

Anger drew him close. Close enough that she saw his dead soul through his icy blue eyes. "She betrayed me with him. After she swore she loved me." Then he went quiet and still. "I wish I'd never started this, but now I can't stop."

Ah, a crack in his armor. "That must have been horrible for you, killing the woman you truly loved."

Sullivan gripped her arm so hard, pain shot down her side. But Ava steeled herself against what he might do next.

"I don't talk about that," he said, pushing her forward again.

"He didn't know she was with you," Ava said, her heart hurting for the evil that had warped this man.

"Well, he figured it out when they found her, didn't he?"

"He's suffered enough."

"Never enough. None of you have suffered. I'm the one who's been through the worst."

Ava got closer, in his face. "If you kill me, it won't matter one bit. He will track you until he finds you."

"No, he won't," Boyd Sullivan said, taking her by the arm to turn her back around to face him. "Because I'm going to kill you, and after he watches and suffers, I'm going to kill him, too."

Ava swallowed the fear trembling through her body.

"You won't do that. You can't keep killing. That will never bring you any satisfaction."

"Shut up."

They'd walked close to a half mile, from her calculations. She prayed that someone would find Roscoe. He wouldn't move until someone came along, and then he'd do his best to follow her trail.

And the trail of a killer.

"Where are we going?" she asked, all the while searching for a way to escape.

"I'll know when we get there," he said.

Ava realized he was stalling. He was waiting for Oliver to show up.

She had to get away, not only to save herself but to protect Oliver, too.

They walked farther down a gully and then back up to a sharp ledge.

"This will do nicely," Sullivan said. "We wait here."

He shoved Ava down against the hard, jagged rocks. "If you make one wrong move, I'll toss you over this ledge."

She didn't respond. She was too intent of figuring out how to push *him* off the ledge.

Roscoe never wavered. The loyal K-9 followed the one scent that he knew with every fiber of his being, that of his partner, Ava Esposito. Even when Nick had called in Chad Watson, a handler who was used to another dog, Roscoe stayed the course.

Oliver remembered Ava always saying that Roscoe was never wrong. He had to believe that, had to cling to that one hope. That they'd find her alive. She'd gotten away from the woman today, even after all the times they'd tried to kill her. Now she had to escape from a madman.

So he prayed for one other thing, too. That somehow they could take down the Red Rose Killer. Then a thought coursed over Oliver.

He'd take Ava alive over capturing the Red Rose Killer.

He didn't want the man to keep killing, but he wanted Ava alive. Period.

When Roscoe stopped and bristled, Oliver and the others stood silent, listening, watching. The very air seemed to still, the humidity so thick Oliver could taste the decay and feel the darkness swirling around them.

Roscoe lifted his nose in the air and held his head up.

The big dog looked back once and then held his head high again.

"We move up," Nick mouthed, Annie silent beside him.

Oliver's whole body screamed in pain. He'd been through all kinds of injuries during his career, but this one cut like a knife through his spine. And yet, he couldn't stop moving because the pain and fear inside his heart hurt even more.

They went off the path and crouched in the heavy bramble deep underneath the tall trees. The woods crackled with a dryness that left Oliver's nostrils covered with dust. Sweat rolled down his forehead and into his eyes, but he had his weapon drawn and his gaze up toward the trees and hills.

Nick flipped his goggles down and then nodded, his fist up for quiet. Taking them off, he offered them to Oliver.

And then Oliver saw them. Ava, sitting on a high bluff beside a man dressed in dark camo, his face covered.

And the man was holding a gun to Ava's side.

Oliver didn't stop to think. He took off around the edge of the hanging ledge, determined to save the woman he loved. When he heard something behind him, he turned and saw a blur of golden fur and felt the rush of wind as Roscoe silently leapt into the air and took off up the steep incline.

Thankful that Chad had ordered the K-9 to go, Oliver followed the dog, each running step slicing a knife-like pain throughout his body. Gritting his teeth, he held steady until he crested the ledge.

But before he could do anything, he watched as Ava rose up and called her partner. "Here, Roscoe. Here."

The big dog barked a reply. Fearful of what Sullivan would do, Oliver shot into the night to distract the killer.

Sullivan whirled, his gun now aimed toward Oliver.

Oliver held his own gun up, but he heard a scream and watched in horror as Ava struggled with Boyd Sullivan. Roscoe leapt up onto the ledge and snarled, his teeth grabbing at Sullivan's camo pants.

Oliver hurried toward Ava and the Red Rose Killer, his gun pointed. "Stop. Let her go!"

The killer screamed in anger, Roscoe still clutching at his pants, and pushed Ava. She fell back, emitting a scream as she went down against the rocky floor of the bluff.

Oliver shot at Sullivan but Sullivan turned and beat at Roscoe with his gun. Roscoe never let go, but then a great ripping sound echoed out over the night. The heavy camouflage material gave way and the killer teetered on top of the ledge, and then with a grunt, his gun firing into the air, Boyd Sullivan fell out of sight and disappeared down into the rocks and bramble below.

Oliver stood there, shocked, and then he started running. "Ava? Ava? Where are you?"

Roscoe barked, looking down below. But then the dog turned to stare at Oliver before turning to run across the bluff's surface.

Oliver watched as Roscoe put his nose down.

The K-9 was touching his nose to the face of the woman who lay still against the rocks. Roscoe whimpered before he turned to give Oliver a plea in the form of a bark.

Oliver heard all of the noise around him and saw the helicopter hovering over them, a spotlight shining like a beacon in the dark. But he kept running toward Ava, the pain in his body forgotten.

When Oliver reached her, Roscoe stepped back and stood silent. Oliver lifted her into his arms, felt her weak pulse and held her there, calling out for the others to get help.

"Hang on, Ava," he said over and over. "You can't give up on me now." When he felt blood on the back of her head, he held her tighter. "Ava, wake up."

"Let us check on her." Chad Watson gently tugged Oliver away.

Soon, the chopper that usually carried Ava and Roscoe to rescue people managed to hover low enough that they got her on a stretcher and took her up so they could get her to the hospital. Roscoe whimpered and came to stand beside where Oliver sat watching, too numb to do anything else.

When Chad came back, he leaned down. "Agent Davison, we need to get you to the hospital, too."

"I'm going down there," Oliver said, pointing to the ravine. "I need to see Boyd Sullivan's body."

Chad shook his head. "Negative, sir. No sign of the Red Rose Killer. He's injured. We found a blood trail, but he's no longer in the area. We're still searching."

A black rage filled Oliver's soul. He let out a grunt full of frustration and failure.

"Don't stop searching," Oliver shouted, trying to stand.

"We won't, sir," Chad replied, calm and in control. "But you need to get help."

Oliver held on to Chad for support. "Yes, get me to the hospital. I'm fine, but I need to be with Ava." Grabbing Chad's protective vest, he said, "You understand, Airman?"

"Yes, sir," Chad replied. "I'll take you there myself."

Ava woke with a soft moan, her mind still lost in the last thing she remembered before Sullivan pushed her. She tried to sit up, to find Roscoe, to see if Oliver was okay.

But she wasn't in the Hill Country woods.

She was in a sterile, dark hospital room.

And her head hurt with all the force of bombs exploding.

"Oliver?" she called, praying he was still alive.

"I'm here," she heard from somewhere in a dark corner.

Then she saw him there, lying on a couch. He stood and hobbled to the chair next to her bed and took her hand.

"You're okay?" she asked, tears burning at her eyes.

"No," he admitted with a weak chuckle. "I hurt everywhere, but they gave me some pain medicine so I'd shut up about you."

She pushed up on the pillow and looked at the contraptions feeding something into a tube in her arm. "What happened? Where's Roscoe?"

"Roscoe is safe and well. Sullivan pushed you and you hit your head. You lost a lot of blood and you have a mild concussion. They told me you might slip into a coma, but I knew you'd wake up."

She held his hand, the warmth and security of having him here giving her strength. "Did we get him? Is Sullivan dead? Or is he behind bars?"

Oliver looked down. "He…he managed to get away, but he's injured. We think he made it to the water and took a boat downriver. We've got people searching and we found several different boats, hidden in various locations."

When she didn't speak, Oliver lifted his head and looked into her eyes. "I'm so sorry."

Seeing the utter dejection in his eyes, Ava asked, "Sorry for what?"

"I let you down. I wanted to end it and I had a chance. I should have gone after him, but I was so worried about you. Roscoe took me to you and I… I couldn't leave you there."

Ava shook her head, thankful that her faithful partner was all right. "You've done everything you can, Oliver. Someone else can take over now. You're battered and bruised and you need to rest. You can rest, with me. With Roscoe. Please tell me you'll do that."

He stared into her eyes, his five-o'clock shadow making him look like a pirate. "I will do that." Then he put his head down against his hands, over her hand. "I'm so tired, and when I thought I'd lost you, I knew I'd been chasing the wrong dream. You're the reason I'm here, and I want to be with you. I'm going to rest, with you and with Roscoe."

"But we won't give up," she said. "We'll keep watch and help the others."

"Yes. But I'm never going in those woods again."

"Me, either," she said. "I think the Gulf Coast is calling my name."

"We'll go there together," he offered. "On our honeymoon."

"Is that a proposal, Special Agent Davison?"

"Is that a yes, Airman Esposito?"

"Yes, yes. Two weeks and I've fallen for you. Forever."

"Roscoe led me to you," he told her between kisses.

"Roscoe is never wrong," she replied with a smile. "He's smart that way," she said, pulling him toward her so she could kiss him. "I'm never avoiding you again."

Oliver held Ava in his arms and kissed her to show her he felt the same way. He couldn't hold back the piercing joy that filled his heart. Ava had renewed his faith in love and hope and all that was good in the world. Whether they took this investigation any further or not, he knew they would stay in each other's lives.

He'd forgotten how to breathe after Madison had died. He'd been carrying around such a heavy guilt, he'd almost been consumed by it. But Oliver had been trying to work his way back to his faith and to God.

And now, because of Ava, he could clearly see the path ahead. That path included being with her the rest of his life.

One week later

The press conference was over.

Ava had watched as Oliver, Justin and Westley handled most of the questions from the media.

Yes, the Red Rose Killer was still out there, but all indications showed he'd left the woods for good this time.

Yes, they had people patrolling the area day and night and the security on base and around the Hill Country had been beefed up.

Yes, they believed the woman who'd been helping

Boyd Sullivan had acted on her own, shooting at them to scare them away, that she possibly could have been the shooter in San Antonio and that she could have been driving the motorcycle but wearing Sullivan's pants. Yes, they believed that both the female shooter and Boyd Sullivan had stolen the car and the motorcycle and tried to run Oliver and Ava off the road and kill them.

No, they didn't yet know who the Anonymous Blogger was, but speculation was rampant that the mysterious woman who had disappeared might very well be the blogger.

No, they had not given up the hunt for the Red Rose Killer. They had BOLOs and ABPs out all over the state of Texas and the entire country.

And finally, Heidi Jenks had tried to ask Oliver where he stood in all of this.

"Special Agent Davison, do you plan to stick around and keep up with the search?"

But before Oliver would answer, Heidi's colleague, John Robinson, shoved her aside, stating he was the lead reporter on this case. "When can I interview you, Special Agent?"

"I'll let you know, since I already know everyone else around here has turned you down."

Robinson had stomped off, but Ava noticed Heidi lingering, her lips tightly drawn in aggravation.

"I think you should give Heidi the interview," she said on a low whisper as they were leaving the conference room.

"I haven't decided to do the interview," Oliver replied. "Besides, I'm still not convinced about Heidi. Despite what everyone else thinks, I suspect she may be the Anonymous Blogger. She's the perfect fit."

"She does seem to resent her colleague," Ava admitted. "But then, John Robinson is a bit snarky and annoying."

"And arrogant," Oliver said, grinning. "But enough about them. We have a trip to Galveston to plan."

They got in Ava's SUV, Roscoe eager to go with them, and headed to the Winged Java. But before they got out, Oliver leaned over and kissed Ava.

"I love you," he said. "I know life with me will be tough. I can't let go of Sullivan and what he did, but I can step back and get my priorities straight while I take a different approach on this investigation. I didn't do that before. Now my future is clear."

"I love you," she replied, her heart swelling because she knew he was sacrificing so much for her. "And I feel the same. I love my work, but at times we'll be far apart. But we can make up for that when we're together."

"And the danger?" he asked, his heart in his eyes.

"The danger is everywhere. We have jobs to do. We have each other. It's a risk I'm willing to take."

"Then it's settled."

He got out and came around to open her door, a gesture that touched Ava. But when they got inside the café, being touched went up several notches to being overwhelmed.

The whole crew was there, smiling and clapping and laughing.

"What's going on?" she asked, surprised to see so many familiar faces.

Oliver sat her down on a chair and, in spite of his still-healing back and leg, got down on one knee, pulled out a little black box and opened it. A diamond ring sparkled and winked at her. When she gasped and looked up, her coworker Chad Watson winked at her, too.

Oliver took the ring and lifted her hand so he could

put it on her finger. "For the record, Airman Esposito, I want everyone here to know I'm going to marry you."

"If she says yes," Chad called out.

"If she says yes," Oliver echoed, his eyes on Ava. They didn't know she'd already said yes, but he wanted her to have this moment.

Ava swallowed the lump in her throat and bobbed her head. "She says yes. She definitely says yes."

Roscoe woofed and stared up at them, a grateful look in his eyes. Because he had known all along. And Roscoe was never wrong.

* * * * *

*The hunt for the Red Rose Killer continues.
Look for the next exciting stories in the
Military K-9 Unit series.*

Mission to Protect—*Terri Reed, April 2018*
Bound by Duty—*Valerie Hansen, May 2018*
Top Secret Target—*Dana Mentink, June 2018*
Standing Fast—*Maggie K. Black, July 2018*
Rescue Operation—*Lenora Worth, August 2018*
Explosive Force—*Lynette Eason, September 2018*
Battle Tested—*Laura Scott, October 2018*
Valiant Defender—*Shirlee McCoy, November 2018*
Military K-9 Unit Christmas—*Valerie Hansen
and Laura Scott, December 2018*

Dear Reader,

Life really does imitate art. When we were writing this series, we heard the news each day. Hurricanes, floods and mass shootings, not to mention other horrible things happening in the world. Sometimes our stories ring true to what can take place in real life. We write to entertain and to enlighten, always offering the promise of the Lord's grace and forgiveness. We don't take that lightly, but with careful prayer and consideration.

This was a tough story to write but we all agreed our portrayal of our military characters had to be handled with care and respect. We wanted to get things right.

I hope I did that with Oliver and Ava's story. Any mistakes are my own. I love and admire our service members and I hope I can bring some honor and glory to what they do every day to keep us safe.

My story has a happy ending and that's why I write romance and romantic suspense. We can never give up on faith, hope and love. I pray you cling to those things even in a world that sometimes is scary and sad.

Until next time, may the angels watch over you, always.

Lenora Worth

Get 4 FREE REWARDS!

We'll send you 2 FREE Books
plus 2 FREE Mystery Gifts.

Love Inspired® Suspense books feature Christian characters facing challenges to their faith... and lives.

FREE Value Over **$20**

SPECIAL EXCERPT FROM

A reporter enlists the help of a soldier and his
bomb-sniffing dog to stay one step ahead of the
bomber who wants her dead.

Read on for a sneak preview of
Explosive Force by Lynette Eason,
the next book in the Military K-9 Unit miniseries,
available September 2018 from Love Inspired Suspense.

First Lieutenant Heidi Jenks, news reporter for CAF News,
blew a lock of hair out of her eyes and did her best to keep
from muttering under her breath about the boring stories
she was being assigned lately.

Heidi shut the door to the church where her interviewee
had insisted on meeting and walked down the steps. She
shivered and glanced over her shoulder. For some reason
she expected to see Boyd Sullivan, as if the fact that she
was alone in the dark would automatically mean the serial
killer was behind her.

After being chased by law enforcement last week, he'd
fallen from a bluff and was thought to be dead. But when
his body was never found, that assumption changed. He
was alive. Somewhere.

Heidi's steps took her past the base hospital. She was
getting ready to turn onto the street that would take her

home when a flash of movement from the K-9 training center caught her eye. Her steps slowed, and she heard a door slam.

A figure wearing a dark hoodie bolted down the steps and shot off toward the woods behind the center. He reached up, shoved the hoodie away and yanked something—a ski mask?—off his head then pulled the hoodie back up. He stuffed the ski mask into his jacket pocket.

Very weird actions that set Heidi's internal alarm bells screaming. She decided it was prudent to get out of sight.

Just as she moved to do so, the man spun.

And came to an abrupt halt as his eyes locked on hers.

Ice invaded her veins. He took a step toward her then shot a look back at the training center. With one last threatening glare, he whirled and raced toward the woods once again.

Like he wanted to put as much distance between him and the building as possible.

Don't miss
Explosive Force *by Lynette Eason,*
available September 2018 wherever
Love Inspired® Suspense *books and ebooks are sold.*

www.LoveInspired.com

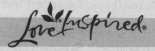
Amos Burkholder looked out over the Millers' fields to be plowed in the spring. He couldn't help but think of them as partly his. Of course, they weren't his fields, and he might not even be here to do the plowing and the planting. But if he was, he would take pride in that work.

Bartholomew Miller appreciated everything he did around the farm, so Amos worked harder than he ever had at home.

Bartholomew had never had a son to help him with all the work around the farm. How had he run this place without sons?

But on the flip side, Amos's *mutter* had been alone doing the house chores, cooking, cleaning and laundry for six men. How did she do it without help?

On the far side of one of the fields, a woman emerged from a bare stand of sycamore trees nestled next to a pond. She walked across the field.

The woman came closer and closer.

Deborah.

Where did she go all the time? She had disappeared every day this week and would be gone for hours. He was about to find out.

With her head down, she didn't see him approaching. He stepped directly into her path a few yards in front of her. When it looked as though she might literally run into him, he cleared his throat.

She halted a foot away. She was so startled to see him there, she appeared to lose her balance. Her arms swung out to keep herself upright.

He reached out and took hold of her upper arms to stop her from tumbling to the ground. "Whoa there."

She gasped. "I'm sorry. I didn't see you."

"Where have you been all day?"

"What? Nowhere." She tried to pull free of his grip, but he held fast.

He shook his head. "You've been somewhere. You've left every day this week and been gone for most of the day."

"I   I went for a walk."

"Where? Ohio?"

"We have a pond just over there. I like to sit and watch the ducks. It's a nice place to think and be alone. You should go sometime."

"I did. Today. You weren't there."

Her self-satisfied expression fell. "I was for a while, then I walked farther."

He sensed there was more to her absence than a walk. "Where?"

"Why do you care?"

"With your *vater* laid up, I'm responsible for everyone on this farm."

"I'm fine. I can take care of myself. May I go now?"

He didn't want to let her go but did. "I don't want you to leave the farm without telling me where you're going."

"Are you serious?"

He gave her his serious look.

She huffed and strode away.

Where did she go every day? He had wanted to follow her, but he realized it was none of his business. But curiosity pushed hard on him. He still might follow her if she didn't obey. Just to see. Just to watch her from a distance. Just to know her secret.

Something inside him feared for her. Feared she would walk out across this field and never return. Feared her secret would consume them both. She was a mystery.

A mystery he was drawn to solve.

Don't miss
Courting Her Secret Heart *by Mary Davis,*
available September 2018 wherever
Love Inspired® books and ebooks are sold.

www.LoveInspired.com

Love Inspired®

Inspirational Romance to Warm Your Heart and Soul

Join our social communities to connect with other readers who share your love!

Sign up for the Love Inspired newsletter at **www.LoveInspired.com** to be the first to find out about upcoming titles, special promotions and exclusive content.

CONNECT WITH US AT:

Harlequin.com/Community

 Facebook.com/LoveInspiredBooks

 Twitter.com/LoveInspiredBks

LISOCIAL2017